She was still a mystery to him,

Harrison fumed.

Isadora. His wife.

She was a wildly passionate woman who set his blood on fire.

A keen-minded con artist who could play poker like a man.

A wily female who had blackmailed him into giving her his name and a year out of his life.

But neither passion nor cunning would ultimately outsmart him, Harrison vowed.

He wasn't sure exactly what the stakes even were between him and his baffling, beautiful new wife. But Harrison swore he would win.

Whatever the cost…

Dear Reader,

As the long summer stretches before us, July sizzles with an enticing Special Edition lineup!

We begin with this month's THAT SPECIAL WOMAN! title brought to you by the wonderful Jennifer Greene. She concludes her STANFORD SISTERS series with *The 200% Wife*—an engaging story about one woman's quest to be the very best at everything, most especially love.

If you delight in marriage-of-convenience stories that evolve into unexpected love, be sure to check out *Mail-Order Matty* by Emilie Richards, book one in our FROM BUD TO BLOSSOM theme series. Written by four popular authors, this brand-new series contains magical love stories that bring change to the characters' lives when they least expect it.

Pull out your handkerchiefs, because we have a three-hankie Special Edition novel that will touch you unlike any of the stories you've experienced before. *Nothing Short of a Miracle* by Patricia Thayer is a poignant story about a resilient woman, a devoted father and a cherished son who yearn for a miracle— and learn to trust in the wondrous power of love.

If absorbing amnesia stories are your forte, be sure to check out *Forgotten Fiancée* by Lucy Gordon. Or perhaps you can't pass up an engrossing family drama with a seductive twist. Then don't miss out on *The Ready-Made Family* by Laurie Paige. Finally, we wrap up a month of irresistible romance when one love-smitten heroine impulsively poses as her twin sister and marries the man of her dreams in *Substitute Bride* by Trisha Alexander.

An entire summer of romance is just beginning to unfold at Special Edition! I hope you enjoy each and every story to come!

Sincerely,

Tara Gavin,
Senior Editor

Please address questions and book requests to:
Silhouette Reader Service
U.S.: 3010 Walden Ave., P.O. Box 1325, Buffalo, NY 14269
Canadian: P.O. Box 609, Fort Erie, Ont. L2A 5X3

LAURIE PAIGE

THE READY-MADE FAMILY

SPECIAL EDITION®

Published by Silhouette Books
America's Publisher of Contemporary Romance

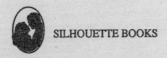 SILHOUETTE BOOKS

ISBN 0-373-24114-3

THE READY-MADE FAMILY

Copyright © 1997 by Olivia M. Hall

LAURIE PAIGE

was recently presented with the *Affaire de Coeur* Readers' Choice Silver Pen Award for Favorite Contemporary Author. In addition, she was a 1994 Romance Writers of America (RITA) finalist for Best Traditional Romance for her book *Sally's Beau*. She reports romance is blooming in her part of Northern California. With the birth of her second grandson, she finds herself madly in love with three wonderful males—"all hero material." So far, her husband hasn't complained about the other men in her life.

Chapter One

It would definitely be a mistake, Isadora Chavez reflected, to fall in love with the man you planned on blackmailing.

The irony inherent in that thought brought a grimace of impatience to her lips. She would never be so foolish.

She refreshed her lipstick, then watched his reflection in the tiny mirror on her compact as Harrison Stone riffled through the papers he'd taken from the wall safe in his office, his handsome face preoccupied and serious.

Earlier, when they'd gone to the community center where she worked as manager, then stayed for a party, he'd been smiling and lighthearted. She wondered how he would react to being blackmailed. She snapped the compact closed and replaced it and the lipstick in her purse.

Staring out at the skyline of Reno etched against the

night sky in colored banners of glittering neon, she reminded herself of all the reasons she was going to do this—*had* to do this—no matter what the consequences.

Isa clenched her hands as misgivings rose like a choking mist inside her. She wondered if a person could be sent to jail for forcing a man into marriage, no matter how justified the act.

It didn't matter. She'd made a promise to her mother, a deathbed promise, to look after Ricky…Rick, as he insisted on being called since he'd become a teenager.

She hadn't done a very good job of keeping that promise.

Her brother was fourteen years old, defiant, headstrong and in custody at a juvenile detention center in Oregon. She had one month left to prove she could provide a stable home for him before the judge made a final decision in the case.

Hearing movement behind her, she turned and faced her escort. Maybe people would think she was his trophy wife.

Except Harrison was only thirty-five, not old enough to need a trophy to add to waning masculinity. His masculinity was in full flower. He was a powerful, virile example of the species.

It was time he took the plunge, she told her conscience, which had a tendency to nag her about truth and honor and all that. As if she didn't have enough worries.

"Isa," he said, demanding her attention in his low, lazy way of speaking, an enticing Western drawl clipped just a bit by back-East schooling.

A tremor of yearning went through her. She loved the way he said her nickname. *Eye-sa.* Soft, drawling, making the two syllables a verbal caress. He'd said her name just like that right before he'd kissed her the first time.

The tremor became a shiver of need fed by a sense of despair and hopelessness. If only things could have been different....

But this wasn't a fairy tale. This was real—life as it had to be lived, not as her foolish heart dreamed it could be.

"Isa? Ready?"

She pulled herself out of the introspective trance. Her course was laid out before her. All she had to do was follow it to the end. She glanced at the papers in his hand.

"Yes," she said, dredging up a smile. "I'm ready." Then she made the mistake of gazing into his eyes.

Harrison had unusual eyes. They had a narrow band of brown around the pupil that turned to dark blue on the outer edge. They were striated with golden strands like tiger's eye—the gemstone, not the animal.

He called them hazel, but that didn't come close to describing their unique coloration. A woman could get lost in those fathomless depths. She sometimes wished she would....

Her heart lurched wildly. She quickly looked away and cleared her throat while waiting for the unreliable organ to settle into a smooth beat once more.

"You seem distracted tonight. Are you having second thoughts about spending the weekend at Tahoe?" He took her arm to lead her toward the door.

She licked her lips and tried to think of a truthful answer that would give nothing away. "And third and fourth ones," she finally admitted. If he only knew!

Instead of chuckling as she'd thought he would do, he laid the papers on his desk and grasped both her upper arms. There was a question in his eyes as he gazed at her.

At five foot nine, she could look most men eye to eye. With Harrison at six-three, she couldn't. For that reason, she'd worn high heels tonight, something she rarely did.

Tilting her head back, she returned his stare, her eyes carefully, artfully blank, an expression perfected by Brigitte Bardot in her early movies. It could hide a multitude of tormented thoughts...or treacherous plans.

"There are no strings attached, you know," he said quite gently. A smile flitted across his mouth.

She wished he'd make love to her right now before all the conniving began, before she was eaten up by guilt, by doubt, by fear. She wished she could forget all the carefully thought-out plans she'd made before she'd moved to Reno from Oregon.

"I know." Her voice was so husky, she had to clear it twice after she said the words. He could be incredibly intuitive about her inner feelings. She reminded herself he was the son of the man who'd cheated her family of its rightful inheritance. In reality, he was a tough, arrogant tycoon.

"You're trembling." He looked puzzled as he rubbed her arms, arousing the longing, the desires that flooded her heart—not just passion, but other, stronger desires for things she couldn't, wouldn't name. They had no place in her schemes.

"I'm a little nervous."

He studied her, a frown notching two faint lines between his eyebrows. "Are you afraid of me?"

She shook her head, then changed her mind. "Maybe. Or myself." She spoke the truth, but felt as if she were reading lines prepared in a script.

"I shake, too, when I think of..." He let the words

trail away into the silence of the office and the whisper of warm air from the overhead vents. "It's powerful, isn't it?"

It wasn't really a question. She nodded anyway.

"I wasn't sure you felt the same." He stroked up and down her arms, causing heat to slither into her abdomen, clustering there like a tiny sun burning out of control. "From the moment I saw you...no, before that. I heard you laugh, and I found myself smiling even though I didn't know the joke."

"At the center..."

"Yes. Your first day there."

Harrison studied the woman he held with such conscious care. He'd never before been as aware of a female in all the ways he was aware of this one. He didn't understand it, and if there was one thing he insisted upon in his life, it was understanding all facets of anything that touched him.

He watched her glance at him, a smile flickering uneasily on her lips, then she looked away, refusing to hold his gaze. She was as elusive as a bird flitting through a forest.

It was one month since they'd met, and he still didn't understand her reserve. Usually women opened up to him immediately. Maybe that's why he found most of them shallow and soon lost interest in their obvious ploys. He mentally shook his head at his uncertainty and confusion over this particular female.

One month. Sometimes it seemed as if he'd been waiting for her. That was how he'd felt the first time he saw her.

The community-center group had thrown a party to welcome her. They'd been delighted to get someone with her experience to take over as manager of the shoestring operation.

Harrison had declined the invitation to attend, but then changed his mind and dropped by to say hello before heading for another meeting. He'd become intrigued the moment he'd entered the building.

He'd heard her laughter—throaty, filled with husky delight, a purr of sound that had whetted his appetite to see the woman. He'd entered the manager's office and stopped dead in his tracks.

Her hair was shiny and black, inherited from a Latino father, he'd later learned, while her skin was porcelain-fair, her eyes green, gifts from her Scottish mother.

She had thick eyelashes, all natural, and brows that arched and lifted like a gull's wing. As tall as a runway model, she walked with a casual feline grace, indifferent to her own charm. He'd gotten hot and bothered the minute he'd seen her. He was that way now.

He'd taken her out to dinner that first night and had seen her nearly every night since. A whole month of going home to bed, but not to sleep. Instead, he lay there and thought about her, his body aching and restless and hard with needs not met.

When she'd agreed to go to his cabin near Lake Tahoe, he'd nearly whooped for joy like a kid.

Now he was afraid she'd change her mind before they could get there. Sometimes he thought she was afraid of him. An odd thought, that. And sometimes she became quiet, withdrawn....

"I wish we were going to be alone at the cabin. I could call and tell everyone I have the flu," he suggested, and was surprised at the wistfulness of his tone.

Hell's bells, did he have a case for her or what? He mocked the feeling but it didn't go away. For the first time in his life, he wanted a woman exclusively to himself with no distractions. It was a little unnerving.

"You have a deal to conclude," she reminded him.

He grimaced. "I know. You know what? I don't give a damn." And for a second, he didn't. Then reality set in.

A year ago, his father had told him the silver mining and jewelry-manufacturing company was in trouble, not because the mine was played out, but because of the slump in the price of silver, a recession in the consumer market, a large debt and poor management. His father had asked for help.

That had been shocking enough, Then, finding out his father was dying of cancer, probably from years of breathing the arid desert dust stirred up by the mining operations, had been the final pull to bring him back here from his mountain home.

Call it filial obligation, stubbornness, whatever, he'd felt duty bound to save the company if he could. After his father died, he'd taken over completely, putting his own successful brokerage business on the back burner in order to do so.

He'd managed to hold things together for the past year. Things were looking up. He'd found a deep-pockets investor.

Then, last month he'd found the woman of his dreams.

He tilted her chin up and gazed into her eyes. Was he the man of *her* dreams? Hard to know. She was such an elusive creature...warm, womanly, solid in his arms...but elusive.

Isa felt her bones go soft at the look he gave her. "I wonder what the other company directors would say to that," she teased, putting them on the solid ground of commerce and reason.

Harrison nuzzled along her temple to her ear. "I don't give a damn about them, either. I want to be alone with you. There are things I'd like to do...."

"What?" she asked, hardly capable of speech but unable to hold the word in. His lips burned her neck with passionate kisses.

"Hold you." He lifted his head. "I know you're an adult woman—you feel that way in my arms—but sometimes you look so innocent, so lost in the world, and I want to..."

"To what?" Her heart pounded as if trying to escape.

He laughed briefly, ironically. "I want to slay dragons for you. Crazy, huh?"

"Not so crazy. Poetic. Heroic, even." She smiled and kept her tone light, but she didn't feel that way.

She'd been eighteen when she'd made that promise to her mother. Nine years she'd lived with it burning before her, a constant goal in her uncertain world. The weight of it sat on her shoulders along with the worry and love she felt for her brother. She wouldn't fall for Harrison's smooth line. But it was hard not to dream of a home filled with love....

When he moved closer, she let herself be gathered in. His body was muscular and warm, a solid wall of strength under her hands as they roamed his chest, then around to his back.

"I could take you right now," he whispered hoarsely. "On the floor, in a chair, standing. It wouldn't matter. Not to me. But I want more than that for you."

The air left her lungs and refused to return.

"When we make love, I want the maximum comfort for you." He paused, tantalizing her with fantasies of them together. "I also want the maximum pleasure. For both of us. It'll be earthshaking."

"What if it isn't?"

He wrapped her closer, so close she could hear his heart beat when she laid her head against him. Against the junction of her legs, she felt the growing hardness to his body. She wanted to answer that call to wild delight, to take him in her until she felt him every-where—inside, outside, a part of her....

"Then we'll practice until it is." He moved swiftly, his lips closing over hers in heady rapture.

She let herself cling to him. His hands rubbed over her, molding her to his hard angles. She swayed against him, side to side, lightly stroking, delirious with plea-sure.

He groaned and cupped her buttocks, holding her still against the solid ridge behind his zipper. His tongue sought hers in passionate play for a long minute before he broke the kiss and rested his forehead against hers.

"Easy, darling," he cautioned, "or else you'll drive me right over the edge of my good intentions."

She stirred her wits, teasing him as she'd done all month to catch and keep his interest. "Good intentions? You have those?"

He frowned in mock displeasure at her, then laughed. "Lots of 'em. Lots and lots." He chuckled at her dis-believing expression.

With the quickness of a lightning bolt, he moved his hands over her, running his palms down her sides and over her hips, outlining her shape as if memorizing it. When they moved upward again and hovered just below her breasts, heat from his hands seared her through the heavy black satin of her dinner dress and jacket.

Fires ignited in her. She arched instinctively against him, wanting more...everything...that instant.

"Let's get out of here," he muttered on a hoarsely drawn breath. "We have a long drive before we get home."

"Home," she repeated. It seemed so right. If only it could be true. If only he would fall in love with her. If only he would ask her to marry him. If only...

She stifled the betraying thoughts. There was no time for dreams that would never be. "Yes, let's go."

She wanted to get the weekend over. She wanted the future, hers and Rick's, settled. Tension pulled like a tightening chain across her forehead as they rode down the elevator from his office to the parking level below the street.

"Music?" he asked. They had taken the highway heading south toward Carson City out of Reno. Now they traveled west toward Lake Tahoe. The road became steep and winding.

"I like the quiet."

"Me, too." He laid a hand briefly on her thigh, then withdrew it to negotiate Spooner Summit. The sign indicated they were 7140 feet high. That was a long way to fall.

She glanced at Harrison's strong profile, then away. It was hard to look at the person who was to be her victim, to make herself be hard and callous toward him.

Like a black widow spider, she lay in wait for him to fall into her web of deceit. As the time drew nearer to execute her deception, she looked at him less and less.

One month, she reminded herself. One month to establish a home and a believable facade of marital happiness in order to convince the judge to put Rick into her custody. One month.

Fear sent a wave of weakness through her. She couldn't even think about failure. This was something she had to do. Rick, for all his insistence that he was a man, was only a boy.

"Relax," a warm, masculine voice advised, a drift of laughter coating the words. Harrison pulled her hands apart and placed her left one palm down on his thigh.

He held it there with his hand over hers. When he had to move it to execute a turn, she left her hand in place.

Through the fine wool of his slacks, she revelled in the warmth and strength of his leg as he pressed the accelerator. She thought of that strength held between her own thighs, of that warmth deep inside her, sharing the passion she'd deliberately set out to induce in him.

A shaky sigh escaped her.

He touched her hand again, and again withdrew it to steer the sleek luxury car around the mountainous curves. Down they dipped into the Tahoe basin, then sped along the eastern shore of the lake and climbed streets slick with frost until he at last turned into the driveway of his cabin.

"Some cabin," she remarked, gazing at a tall, three-car garage structure with redwood siding and decking all around.

He grinned like a boy showing off a treasure.

"It's lovely," she said after he parked and they started up the enclosed stairs from the garage to the main floor of the house. It was built into the side of the mountain.

"I'll give you the grand tour in the morning," he said. He glanced at his watch.

So did she. It *was* morning. One o'clock on a cold morning in April. April the third. At least it wasn't April Fool's Day. She didn't think she could have pulled off her hoax on the famous trickster day. It would have been too macabre.

"The snow will be crusty in the morning. That'll make the skiing tougher. Perhaps we'll wait for the afternoon when it softens up a bit."

Spring slush. That's what she and her friends had called the snowpack as the sun grew hotter and the snow became heavy with water. It clumped on top of the skis, making turns difficult and putting the knees at greater risk.

"It's been a while since I've skied," she remarked while he unlocked the door and stepped inside to punch a code into the burglar alarm.

"It'll come back. We'll take it easy, let you get your ski legs under you before we tackle the advanced slopes." He held the door wide. "Enter," he invited with a sweep of his hand.

She stepped across the threshold, and he closed the door, locking out the cold. The house was already warm.

"Do you leave the heat on all the time?" she asked, curious about how often he came up here.

"No. I call ahead and let my neighbor know when I'm coming in. She and her son take care of things when I'm not here."

Isa murmured a hum of understanding. It sounded as if he had nice neighbors. During the past month she'd noticed he seemed to be well-liked by the people she'd met. But then, he wouldn't introduce her to his enemies, and a business tycoon had to have a few of those.

"The house is on three levels," he explained. "The living room, kitchen and den are here. The bedrooms are one floor up, the rec room and basement one floor down. Firewood is stored down there, too. There's a dumbwaiter to bring it up."

"How convenient." She couldn't quite hide the sarcastic edge as she thought of the apartments she'd lived in most of her life. Any one of them would have fit on a single floor here.

He cast her a sharp, assessing glance.

She kept her face that perfect blank she'd learned so well while listening to her father's schemes. He'd grown angry if she expressed concern or pointed out flaws in his plans. She'd learned to keep her opinions to herself.

"I'll show you to your room, then bring the luggage up."

"Thank you. I am rather tired." There, maybe he would accept that old excuse for her short temper. Truthfully, she was beginning to feel somewhat ravaged. Fighting a constant war with one's own conscience was exhausting.

He led the way up another flight of steps to the top level. Her bedroom was on one side of a wide hall surrounding the stairwell. A sky bridge connected the hall to a double set of doors on the other side of the house. The master suite, she assumed, and felt her scalp prickle.

"You have your own bathroom," Harrison told her. "There are two bedrooms and a connecting bath across the hall."

"Umm." She sounded breathy and reedy.

"Come see the view," he invited, not bothering to turn on the bedroom lights.

His voice had dropped into a lower, sexier register, sending a clenching sensation along her nerves. She let him usher her to the wide set of windows on the opposite wall, his hand lightly touching her back.

The moon cast a silvered path over the lake while lights glittered like magic pearls strung around the shore. Amid the dark stands of evergreen trees, snow reflected the moonlight like drifts of fairy dust in a dreamscape.

The scene was so beautiful it brought tears to her eyes. With them came the despairing sadness she'd felt when her mother died and all the joy had disappeared from her life.

"It always gets to me, too," he murmured, resting his head against hers, his arm encircling her waist.

She sensed the wonder he felt and knew it was the same as hers. Standing there looking at the play of moonlight on the mountains and lake, she made a poignant discovery—to share a beautiful thing made it even more wonderful.

His hands exerted but little pressure on her, only enough to nudge her into turning toward him. She pivoted slowly, as if in a dream. The tears pressed harder.

He cupped her face, then slipped his hands into her hair and lifted her mouth to his. She clutched his suit jacket, her hands creasing the fabric as she struggled against sensations she had no right to feel. Emotions only got in the way.

Blackmailers must be ruthless.

His lips touched hers. The kiss reached inside and plucked her heartstrings until she quivered with longing.

Blackmailers must be coldhearted.

Still holding the kiss, he opened his jacket, inviting her inside. She hesitated, then slipped her arms around him, knowing there was only the smooth cotton of his shirt between her hands and his skin. Thoughts spiraled off like the meteor trails of fireworks.

Blackmailers must be clear-thinking.

Feeling the threat of incipient softheadedness, she gave a little keening moan and tore her mouth from the sweet wonder of his. She pressed her face against his shirt.

He reached between them, pulled his tie free, then unbuttoned his shirt. He did the same to the black satin jacket that matched her dress. "Don't stop now," he whispered.

"I…we shouldn't…. It's…too soon."

"No," he denied. "It's perfect, just us and the moon and the stars, the beauty of the mountains."

She tried to think. She *had* to think. There were things she had to do, important things. But for now...for this one night...couldn't she forget her plans and have just one night?

But of course she couldn't. For one thing, her conscience wouldn't let her accept the sweet mindlessness of total pleasure with the man she intended to blackmail. For another, it was too dangerous. If everything worked as she'd planned, by the end of this weekend trip, she'd be his wife.

Chapter Two

"Come with me," Harrison whispered urgently. The house was two years old. No woman had been in his quarters. He wanted this one to be the first. Maybe the only one...

He was startled at the thought. What was he thinking of? Or was he thinking at all? Good question.

Maybe he'd better let things calm down before he found himself saying things he might regret in the morning. He'd always prided himself on keeping a cool head. He wasn't going to lose it now. All he had to do was douse the fire in his blood with some rational thought.

"Perhaps we'd better think on this." Her voice was a wisp of sound in the dark, enchanted night.

"I don't want to think," he muttered, nuzzling along her temple, excited by the scent of her. "I just want to hold you and kiss you and make love to you."

So much for rational thought, he told himself, mocking his own runaway libido. Next thing he knew, he'd be down on one knee saying a lot of sappy things the way the heroes did in the spate of mushy romantic comedies that had hit the movies recently.

He lifted his head and stared down at the wealth of shiny black hair that hid her face from view as she pressed her forehead to his bare chest.

Heaven help him. He couldn't believe he'd ripped his shirt open so he could feel her touch directly on his skin. That was a primitive reaction to lust. He prided himself on being a modern man. Enough of this. He had to regain control.

Then he felt her lips touch his bare skin.

An electric bolt sizzled through him. He wanted to pick her up in his arms and run to his room. He might let her out in a year.

Forcing himself to practicalities, he set her away from him and cleared the huskiness from his throat. "I'd better see to our luggage."

She nodded and turned away before he could catch more than a glimpse of her face in the moonlight pouring in the window. She laid her purse on the nearby table, then sat in the chair next to it, her arms wrapped across her waist as if she'd been taken with a sudden chill.

There was something mournful in her still figure. He wanted to comfort her as well as kiss her. An odd sensation.

He hurried out while he still could.

Isa woke to a radiant morning. The snow reflected the sun from every mountain peak, every pine and fir tree as far as the eye could see. She was blinded by its brilliance.

A blue jay complained as a crow pushed him off the ledge of a bird feeder next door. He flew up to the pine branch outside her window and cawed loudly.

She yawned and stretched, but didn't jump out of the warm bed the way she usually did. Instead, she lay beneath the comforter and thought of the previous evening.

Harrison had brushed her cheek tenderly after bringing up her suitcase and placing it on an old-fashioned cedar chest. He hadn't kissed her again, although she'd expected it.

She'd expected more than kisses. She'd thought she'd have to refuse him, even though part of her had wanted the lovemaking.

Odd. She'd thought he'd wanted it, too.

But he'd resisted the temptation and left her with a smile that had been as troubling as it had been mysterious. She'd somehow lost control of the situation.

A knock on the door caused every nerve in her body to jump. "Yes?" she managed to call in a fairly steady voice.

"Ready to try the slopes? The ski report is good. A dusting of fresh snow fell during the wee hours."

"I'll be down in twenty minutes," she promised, and flung the covers back. She made it in sixteen minutes flat.

Harrison was in the kitchen sipping a cup of coffee when she arrived. "Cereal is in the cabinet over the coffeemaker," he advised. "There's milk in the refrigerator."

"Thanks." She helped herself.

Looking at the clock, she realized she'd slept until nine. "Have you been up long?"

"Hours. I didn't sleep well last night. Did you?"

She glanced his way and saw the irony in his smile.

And the hunger in his eyes. Heat radiated inside her. "Actually, I did. The last thing I remember was looking at the moonlight on the mountains and thinking how beautiful it all was."

In the moment before she fell asleep it had seemed that all things were possible—marriage, security, happiness.

After eating, they tugged on ski clothes and headed for the chairlift. Harrison wore jeans with his boots, but she preferred the warmth of ski bibs, which were made like bib overalls. She wore a ski parka. Harrison wore a windbreaker over a cotton turtleneck and a wool sweater.

They were on their way to the top of the mountain by ten. Around them, couples called to each other, making arrangements to meet later for lunch.

"College kids from Davis or Sacramento up for the weekend," Harrison decided, watching them with an indulgent expression.

"They look so young," she murmured, envious of their joy and seemingly uncomplicated lives.

She wondered how her escort would be with children. An easy touch? No, firm but fair would most likely be his style. She looked away when his gaze shifted toward her.

It was strange, but she felt so vulnerable today, as if all her innermost thoughts were strung out like clothes on a line for anyone to see.

"And you're so old? I've been wondering if I should have asked for a note from your mommy before bringing you up here for the weekend." There was a question in his voice.

"I'm twenty-seven." She was surprised that he might have thought she was as young as the couples around them.

"That makes me eight years older."

"I knew you were thirty-five." She pressed her lips together but the words were already spoken.

"Ah, you asked questions about me," he murmured, leaning close to her. "I like that."

The chair swung back and forth. They were about thirty feet above the ground. "Don't move," she said.

He laughed. "Now I know your weakness—you're scared of heights."

"Only when my feet aren't on the ground."

"My feet aren't on the ground at all when I'm around you," he told her in a deep, sexy drawl.

Her heart knocked around a bit. She summoned the teasing repartee that had caught his interest earlier. "You've always looked pretty solidly planted to me."

"Then we'll have to change your perception." He leaned over and kissed her on the mouth just before they had to lift their ski tips at the end of the ride.

They spent two hours on the slopes, stopped at the lodge for lunch, then went back up. Thoughtfully, he stayed on easy, intermediate runs with her. The snow turned slushy as the day wore on. The third time she caught her ski tip and went down for the count, he decided to call it a day.

"You're tired. There's no reason to overdo it. There will be other days to play," he added, giving her a flirtatious smile while he waited for her to get up. He pushed one of her ski poles within reach as she got herself back together.

She brushed snow off her face, laughing and shivering when a clump went down her neck. Sitting on the cold ground, she looked up at Harrison Stone.

Silhouetted against the afternoon sun, he looked powerful, a man filled to the brim with the energy of life.

A force to be reckoned with...and she wanted to do the reckoning.

Her smile died as she thought of the things she had to do. At this moment, he was looking at her with amused tenderness. Unless he confessed undying love and demanded marriage today, tomorrow he'd look at her with hatred in his hazel eyes.

He gave her a hand up, then brushed the snow off her ski bib and out of her hair. "What dark thought crossed your fascinating mind just then?" he inquired with mock concern.

She adjusted her sunglasses, pointed her skis downhill and pushed off. "That I can beat you to the lodge," she yelled back and bent into the turn, taking a narrow trail through the trees.

He stayed behind her until the last thirty yards, then he passed her easily. He was waiting, skis off, when she cruised to a stop, breathless from the fast run.

"If you want to make some black diamond runs, I'll wait," she volunteered.

"Actually, I was thinking of heading in and trying out the hot tub. After those last two falls, you might need some—"

She hit him with a snowball before he could finish the sentence, then picked up her skis and dashed toward the parking lot before he could retaliate. He muttered a few choice words while digging snow out of his jacket collar.

When they were on their way to his house, she explained. "I just couldn't stand it, you looking so pristine and all. I mean, you didn't fall once. You deserved a little snow in the face."

"Yeah, thanks. You'd better watch your back, is all I have to say on the subject."

She wondered what form his revenge would take and

envisioned all sorts of wonderful scenarios. She shivered delicately.

At the house, he directed her to leave her skis, boots and poles in the garage with his. "The hot tub is on the deck outside my bedroom. Come join me when you're ready."

She nodded and hurried to her room. She changed to her bathing suit, then hesitated. What if he wasn't wearing one?

Should she?

The question echoed through her head with every beat of her heart. She looked at her one-piece suit in the mirror. It was cut high enough on the legs and low enough at the neckline to be interesting without being outrageous.

She pulled on a thick terry robe she found in the closet. Harrison thought of everything for his guests. That depressed her, somehow. On this note, she went to find him.

Crossing the sky bridge to his bedroom gave her an odd feeling. She clutched the banister like a lifeline as she made the journey that might seal her fate for better or for worse.

His door was open.

She walked in. The first thing she saw was the king-size bed covered in a black, brown and blue Indian-print blanket. Four pillows in matching pillowcases leaned invitingly against the headboard. A book on Scotland was close at hand on the night table by the bed.

The second thing she noticed was his clothing tossed across a chair near the bed. Compared to the men she'd known, Harrison was a very neat person.

"Out here," he called to her.

The French doors that opened onto the deck framed

the same view of mountains and lake that her windows did. He'd left one door ajar for her. She went out and closed it behind her.

The frothing water covered him up to his neck and hid his body from her perusal. She looked away when she saw him noting the direction of her gaze. Laying the robe on a deck chair, she took a tentative step down into the tub. A hand grasped her ankle. She gasped and tried to pull back.

Too late. She fell with a clumsy thrashing of her arms. He caught her against him as he stood. As she grabbed at him wildly, she realized he, too, was wearing a swimsuit.

"Ah, what have we here?" he demanded philosophically. Revenge sparkled in his hazel eyes. "A damsel in distress, I think. Perhaps she's afraid she'll be dunked in a boiling cauldron or some such fate."

"Oh, please, sir, don't drop me. I'll do anything if only you won't drop me," she pleaded prettily.

"Anything?" His dark eyebrows arched upward.

"Anything."

He didn't speak for so long she was forced to look at him. The playfulness disappeared as his mood shifted in some way she couldn't read. He held her gaze while his eyes went darker.

"What?" she asked, sounding breathless.

He sank into the steaming, bubbling water until it covered them to their necks. "This," he said in a husky voice as warm as the water that surrounded them, and kissed her.

She realized all the time they'd spent together that day had been but the preliminary for this moment. They had chased each other down the mountain, had laughed and teased and insulted each other's form, had eaten the food served in the lodge while a hunger for more exciting fare built in them. Now that desire blazed bright and strong between them, demanding to be unleashed.

In her heart and body, she was ready for this, for him. Only her conscience flayed her with misgivings. She closed her eyes and ignored it.

With his lips moving over hers, even the voice of doom and gloom was soon silenced. With a throaty cry, she wrapped her arms around his shoulders and returned the kiss with all the pent-up longing in her heart.

Passion bubbled around them like the frothy water, adding to the tumult she felt inside. His hands roamed over her, then paused at the straps of her bathing suit. He slipped his fingers under the material and slowly peeled it off her shoulders.

A chant began inside her, urging her to take all the moment offered. She sighed as she lifted one arm and let the strap slide over it, then the other.

He stroked the sensitive skin above her breasts with his fingertips, exerting no pressure but sending showers of sensation over her. Rising, he moved up one step so that the water lapped midway between their waists and shoulders.

"You're very beautiful," he told her. His fingers dipped between her breasts, tracing a path along the bone, edging the top of her suit downward. The material hung suspended on the very tips before he slid his hands over her completely.

She drew in a sharp breath as he lifted one breast clear of the bubbles and kissed the mounded curve before moving farther down, opening his hand so he could reach the pebbled nipple with his mouth.

He sucked gently at the tip before stroking it with his tongue. She arched against him, unable to control the hunger his touch set off. He moved his hands to her back and pulled her against him.

"When you move against me...yes, like that," he whispered when she pressed against him, no longer aware of her movements, but reacting instinctively. "It drives me wild. All I can think of is being in you...moving with you...."

"Yes...yes..."

"Is that what you want?" He kneaded her breasts, then laved them again with his tongue, driving her mad with his circling and stroking and teasing.

"Yes." She could only sigh the word.

He caressed her for a long time, his kisses slow, almost languid, as they explored the passion between them.

Isa ignored the warnings that rose and burst in her mind like the bubbles on the frothing water. Tomorrow would be time enough for regrets.

When he took hold of her hips and guided her across his lap until she straddled him, she didn't protest.

He drew her to him, pressing for greater intimacy. Slowly he shifted her against him, drawing the maximum pleasure from her. She bit lightly, carefully into the flesh of his shoulder, holding on as sensation burst over her.

"I knew it would be this way," he muttered, kissing her eyebrow, her nose, the side of her mouth.

"How?" she asked, filled with the sweet wonder of it.

"Magic. It's been there from the first moment. I've thought about you here, like this, just the two of us, with the world at our feet...."

Her heart was beating so hard she thought it would explode right out of her. It had to be the same for him. She felt him shudder when she pressed against him, moving lightly, hovering like a hummingbird, then pressing again.

He caught her around the waist and lifted her away. "Let's get out of here." He stood, then swung her from the bubbling tub and set her on her feet.

The cold air hardly had time to envelop her before she was engulfed in the thick robe. He urged her into the house. He grabbed a huge bath towel from a stack by the door and dried her face and hair, then himself.

They gazed at each other without speaking. He pushed the robe and suit from her. The garments pooled around her feet. They stood without moving.

The moment crystallized around them, one perfect moment in time that she wanted to capture and keep forever.

"I'm afraid to touch you," he said hoarsely. "You might disappear the way you've done each night in my dreams."

She was afraid, too. Passion was a fool's game. She had to be clearheaded and ruthless, not weak and gullible as women often were about men and love.

He sucked in an audible breath, held it, let it go. It was as if the act freed him to move. He swept her against him. With one hand, he stripped the covers from the bed. Gently, his gaze never wavering from hers, he laid her there.

He smoothed the hair from her forehead. "Let me take care of things first. I won't want to stop once I join you."

For a second she didn't realize what he meant, not until he shucked his suit and reached into the bedside drawer.

"Oh," she murmured and then felt foolish as he gave her a quick perusal.

His eyes darkened. He stood very still for a thoughtful few seconds. "This is probably a stupid question, but you have done this before, haven't you? I mean, sometimes you have this way of looking so innocent..."

Embarrassment flooded her. "I was engaged once, during my last year of college."

His concern gave way to sympathy. "What happened?"

"Well, my father died and I had to take care of my brother. My fiancé decided he didn't want a ready-made family."

"You were lucky to be rid of him," Harrison said in a low, growly voice. "You made it on your own."

She looked away, reminded of her deception once more.

He swooped down beside her, his long, powerful body stretched out beside hers, one leg covering her as if to keep her from escaping. "Don't," he whispered and rained kisses on her face wherever they might fall.

"Don't what?" she managed to ask before she was completely drawn into the rapture again.

He tilted her chin up so he could study her face. "Don't be afraid. Sometimes you seem so lost and worried—like now—I want to tuck you in my pocket like a stray kitten and take you home."

She smiled, but not with gladness. "And so you have. I'm in your home."

"And my bed," he added huskily. "I've dreamed of this moment for a month. Have you?"

"I've thought about us, about a lot of things," she answered truthfully. "But this wasn't part of the plan." She froze, but he didn't seem to catch the slip.

"Now it's time to make those dreams a reality."

He bent to her mouth. She turned her head.

"Isa?"

"I think I'd better go to my room," she said unsteadily. This wasn't supposed to be happening. She had to be in control. She pushed against his chest. "Please, let me go. You don't know.... I can't. Not now. Not like this."

The panic surprised her, coming unbidden and sliding over her like a turbulent fog. Harrison held her without speaking. He seemed to be waiting.

She felt new and tender, like a young plant just sprouted. A transplanted one. Would she thrive here in the high Nevada desert, or would the harsh environment destroy her?

Finally, he nuzzled his face against the side of hers. She held very still, swallowing the tears that insisted on forming.

"What's wrong?"

"I need to go...."

"Why?"

"It's too soon," she finally whispered. "I'm not... this isn't like me."

He chuckled and nuzzled her some more. Against her body, she felt the press of desire in him and the ready answer in herself. She shuddered as longing grew in her.

"It's confusing," he admitted, "to want someone like this. I've never felt this way before."

"You haven't?" She flinched at the naive wonder in the question. She couldn't decide if he was the most accomplished rogue she'd ever met or if he meant what he said.

"No." He turned and lifted her at the same time, settling her over his long, muscular body.

Almost nose to nose, she gazed into his eyes, wondering if he could possibly be falling in love with her. She wanted to ask, but didn't. In the grand scheme of things, it didn't matter. In fact, it might make everything worse.

Reason returned, and with it, the memory of the carefully laid plans she'd made. She had to stick to her chosen path.

That was her life—a road laid out before her, filled with promises and schemes she couldn't forget. Her brother's future depended on her. She had to do this for him.

"You're mournful again," Harrison murmured. He stroked her back, his touch gentle and soothing. "What's wrong?"

Her heart lurched. Did he suspect...? He surely didn't, or he wouldn't be lying beneath her with that lambent gleam in his eyes. She hadn't given herself away. She was sure of it.

"Nothing." She bent her head and dropped kisses along his collarbone, then up the cords of his neck. When he would have held her, she slipped away and fled to her room.

Harrison heard a stair creak, then saw a shadow pause outside the kitchen door. His pulse rate doubled as he realized Isa was up. Finally. It was almost ten.

He went to the doorway, a smile he couldn't suppress on his face. Picture of a dope, he mocked himself. It did no good. The smile wouldn't go away. He couldn't even tone it down.

"Hi," he said.

Isa hovered like a nervous cat in strange territory on the last step. She looked gorgeous in a silky white shirt with full sleeves, worn outside black slacks with a gold belt. Gold hoop earrings swung from her ears.

He went to her, then glanced back over his shoulder to make sure they were out of sight of the kitchen. They were.

"I've missed you," he murmured for her ears alone,

then kissed her. He meant to keep it light, but that was impossible.

Her lips trembled under his, then opened to let him inside. She didn't melt into him as she'd done last night. In fact, she didn't touch him in any way, other than the mouth-to-mouth contact. He drew back, wondering what had happened to the woman who'd kissed him so ardently, then rushed to her room as if afraid of the passion between them.

"I wish you had stayed the night," he told her. "My bed felt lonely after having you there."

She smiled but didn't look at him. "I thought we'd better get some sleep. You have business to take care of. Do you have a visitor?" Her gaze strayed past him toward the kitchen.

"Yes, Ken Martin, the company controller, is here with the final reports for the contract. I'll need to go over them."

A bunch of dry numbers was the last thing he wanted to think about. In fact, after getting a whiff of Isa's sweet scent, all he wanted to do was head back to bed.

Down, boy, he chided himself. He'd get the business out of the way, then maybe he and Isa would have the rest of the day...and night...for each other.

Odd. He'd never considered letting a woman take precedence over a deal before, but with this one...hell, she was all he thought about.

She stirred restlessly, and he stepped back. She walked into the kitchen, her face an odd mixture of haunting sadness and a carefully controlled smile.

A stage smile.

The thought startled him. It didn't look false, yet he knew it wasn't quite real, but something she assumed for social purposes. He didn't even know how he knew that.

He watched her as he introduced her to the company financial wizard. Her expression didn't vary. Her smile was warm, her remarks casual but designed to put another at ease. He saw Ken, who was usually awkward around women, fall for her charm.

The odd thing was, he couldn't tell whether she was sincere with Ken or not. She was an enigma, that was for sure.

Recalling how her lips had trembled under his a moment ago and how she had responded to him last night, he wondered why she'd insisted she had to return to her room after their impromptu and incomplete lovemaking. He'd wanted to sleep with her.

And that was the oddest thing of all. From not having a woman at his private retreat he'd gone to wanting this one beside him all night. He'd wanted to wake with her.

Whoa, he cautioned himself. Don't go off the deep end. He wanted to know more about this woman who attracted him as no other ever had.

Her throaty laughter broke into his musings. Ken must have said something funny. The Wiz, as they called him, was looking vastly pleased with himself. Isa laughed as if delighted with the conversation.

Harrison felt a tiny jolt of...of... Nah. He couldn't be jealous. He'd never been jealous of a woman in his life. He wasn't going to start now.

Chapter Three

Isa pulled on a jacket and wandered out onto the deck. On the main level, she could walk around three sides of the cabin. Curious, she peered into each room as she ambled by. Kitchen, dining room, living room with fireplace. She'd seen those.

Harrison hadn't given her the grand tour as he'd promised. He and his expert had been too busy...all day. They hadn't even stopped for lunch. It was late afternoon, and she was restless.

Seeing books along one wall of a room, she stopped by the door. The temptation was too much. She loved to read, and she couldn't resist the opportunity to see what his tastes were.

Opening the door, she went inside.

"We're in a meeting."

She jumped at the irritated tone and spun around. Harrison and Ken, their expressions preoccupied, looked up from a desk spread with papers and charts. She felt like a mouse that had stumbled into a convention of cats. Her host was the boss of this particular gang and the one who'd snapped at her.

"Oh, I'm sorry. I didn't realize anyone was in here." She grappled for the doorknob.

"Wait," Harrison commanded, his tone going from icy and gruff to warm and husky. "Sorry to growl. I wasn't expecting anyone—the perils of having a gorgon for a secretary. She wouldn't let the devil himself into my office during a meeting."

Isa pulled her ragged composure around her and resorted to the teasing humor she used with him. "Because he's already present?" she suggested, giving him a bold once-over.

Her quip drew a snort of surprised laughter from Ken, the financial genius. People didn't talk to Harrison Stone like that and get away with it, she surmised.

Well, she was just full of surprises, and the biggest one was still to come.

Harrison's eyes crinkled attractively at the corners as he, too, chuckled. He came to her. His hand on her arm stopped her departure. He reached around and closed the door she'd just opened.

"You'll pay for that smart remark," he promised. "Later."

A thrill of longing coursed through her. She fought to maintain her equilibrium. Blackmailers had to be tough. They couldn't fall for sexy smiles and bedroom eyes.

"Stay." He gestured toward the wall of books. "Help yourself. There's an easy chair that's made for reading. It's one of my favorites." Now he was all charming host, seeing to her comfort and entertainment.

"That's okay. I can fend for myself. I'm not a child that has to be indulged or entertained."

Keeping her expression neutral, but pleasant, she let him guide her to the leather recliner and remove her jacket. He laid it over the arm of a matching chair.

"Believe me, I don't think of you as a child." His smile was purely male.

She settled in the chair while he leaned over the polished walnut table between the two easy chairs and turned a three-way reading lamp to its brightest setting. He pointed out the button so she could adjust the recliner to the angle she wanted. Then he went back to his desk and the work there.

"Now," Ken said, resuming their conversation, "I've found a better supply of turquoise, so we're okay on that."

Isa selected a book on birds of North America and silently leafed through it while listening to the conversation from the other end of the room. The two men were totally engaged in the business of wheeling and dealing.

Any illusions she might have cherished about having a special place in Harrison's life had been dispelled by his abrupt reaction to her interruption.

That was good. She'd needed to be reminded that life was real. Illusions had no place in her plans.

At six, she drifted into the kitchen and looked through the cabinets and refrigerator. Apparently Harrison didn't allow time for eating when engrossed in contracts and such.

She found some frozen pasta and green beans. That was a start. A can of crabmeat. A bottle of white Chablis. Ah. She had the makings of a meal.

While the pasta was heating in the microwave oven,

she prepared a cream sauce, added the can of crabmeat, sprinkled in some Parmesan cheese and *voilà!*

"Dinner," she yelled down the hall at seven.

The two men arrived almost before the word died away. "I meant to take you out tonight," Harrison said rather sheepishly. "You've been a sport today." He brushed a kiss across her forehead as she passed him with the bowl of green beans.

Ken stared in shock at this display. Apologizing even in a roundabout way obviously wasn't the boss's style.

The men washed up in the utility room next to the kitchen. She'd already set the dining room table and brought the food in. On an impulse, she lit the four candles in a crystal candelabra and placed it in the center of the table.

When Ken and Harrison appeared, she took the hostess position at the table and smiled graciously. "Gentlemen, please be seated."

She watched Harrison's expression to see how he would handle her taking over like this. To her relief, he merely grinned and took his place to her right. Ken sat in the remaining chair.

Isa picked up a fork when the men were settled. They began on the salads. After eating the pasta dish, the green beans with sesame seeds and hot rolls, she served coffee and warm cookies, also found in the plentiful freezer.

Harrison leaned toward her, his wineglass raised in a salute. "To a delightful and multitalented guest."

His eyes left no doubt in her mind about which talents he referred to. Warmth crept around her heart. She looked away from his admiring gaze.

"Hear, hear," Ken echoed. They drank to her.

"Well, back to work. We should be finished in another hour," Harrison told her when they'd eaten. "Leave the dishes. I'll take care of them later."

After he and his controller left, she cleaned the kitchen by herself and went to her room to prepare for bed. So much for getting to a man's heart through his stomach....

Harrison slipped through the hall like a sneak thief in his stocking feet. It was almost midnight. Isa had been a jewel all day. A forebearing one. Most women demanded all a man's time and attention, especially on a weekend at a mountain retreat.

That was probably why he'd never brought anyone up here. He didn't have many moments to spare for the required mating rituals that females demanded. Except Isa didn't make demands.

She didn't need attention every minute, either. She could amuse herself. And she could cook. Yeah, she was a paragon of womanly talents. All of which he liked.

Coming to her door, he paused, then knocked as quietly as he could. He'd hoped she would wait up for him. The need to see her was strong. He fought a battle with himself and lost.

He tried the knob and found the door unlocked. He slipped inside and waited for his eyes to adjust to the dark.

Going to the bed, he stopped beside it. She was asleep, one arm curled over her head, the other across her rib cage. The covers were tucked neatly over her breasts.

The moonlight highlighted the curve of her prominent cheekbones and the smoothness of her brow. She looked incredibly young and vulnerable in her long-sleeved nightgown, her hair spread over the pillow like black silk.

Desire tore at him. Oddly, not all of it was sexual. There were other emotions mixed in. He hadn't had the time to get involved with a woman in years, not since his college sweetheart had gone home for Christmas vacation and returned engaged to a senator's son.

He smiled. He'd taken it hard at the time, but later, he'd been glad. She'd turned into a nagging shrew, he had heard.

Suppressing the urge to climb under the covers with the sleeping beauty, he turned and padded out, going down the hall to his moonlight-flooded room and memories of holding her.

Isa opened her eyes when she was sure Harrison was gone. Her heart had nearly leapt out of her chest while he'd stood there watching her. It had taken all the control she could summon to feign a deep and peaceful slumber.

After waiting a half hour, she couldn't stand the suspense another minute. If she was going to act, she'd better get on with it. Before her nerve ran out.

Reminding herself of all the reasons she was carrying out this dangerous plan, she dressed in black. Taking a tiny flashlight from her purse, she tiptoed down the stairs to the study Harrison had used earlier.

Thank goodness he was such an organized person. The contract was lined up on his desk, along with the various reports Zeke Merry had demanded. If what she'd learned the past month was true, the crotchety old man would walk out of a deal if every single detail wasn't to his liking.

Unless he married her, Harrison would find out how Mr. Merry reacted to the contract being cancelled.

All the doubts she'd ever felt dropped on her shoulders. It took more energy to be a thief than she'd ever realized.

Without giving herself time to consider further, she scooped the contract and reports into a black nylon case. She laid some paper out to replace the items in case Harrison noticed the real stuff was missing before she was ready for him to do so.

Feeling like a snake, she slithered back up the stairs to her room. Now where could she hide the nylon bag until she could make good on her proposition for him?

Her bedroom would be the first place Harrison checked, so her suitcase was out. In the shower, she decided. She'd hang it over the showerhead. No one would think of looking there.

So how come she had?

Better try someplace else. An obvious place. That was least noticed, she'd once read. Hide in plain sight.

Where was an obvious place no one would ever think to look?

Under the mattress, of course.

Ha. Ha. Very brilliant.

After another ten minutes of considering, she followed her instincts and hung the bag in the back of the closet. There in the shadows no one would notice it, even in daylight. Maybe.

At one, she crept back into bed, but no matter how many sheep she tried to count, they kept turning into shiny metal bars...prison bars. She got up and moved the incriminating evidence twice.

As the sun backlit the eastern edge of the mountains, Isa put on a pot of coffee. Clouds were moving in from the west. She wondered if that meant snow or rain.

"Good morning."

Every muscle in her body jumped. She jerked around to face Harrison. She could feel the blood drain from her face. She must look as guilty as a deacon caught in a bawdy house.

"Sorry. I didn't mean to startle you." His smile was slow and easy. "You're up early."

Her blood circulated again as she realized he wasn't going to attack her and demand to know what she'd done with the loot.

"Yes. I'm not usually a morning person."

"Aren't you?" His softly drawled question added other shades of meaning to the words, layer upon layer, as if they had been lovers a long time. As if they were real lovers.

His eyes gleamed as he gave her a thorough once-over that left her trembling like an aspen leaf. She was acutely aware that over her nightgown she wore the same robe he'd wrapped around her after their sojourn in the hot tub. She hadn't expected him to be up at this time of the day after working so late.

"No, but it is rather nice to greet the day when everything is all fresh and..." She'd started to say *pure*, but that didn't seem quite appropriate. "And new."

She refocused on her task and turned the water off. She carefully poured every drop into the coffeemaker and flipped the switch. In a few seconds, its friendly gurgle filled the tense silence of the kitchen.

No, only she was tense. Harrison had a lazy grin plastered on his face. What was he so pleased about, anyway?

But then, why shouldn't he be pleased? He'd lived a life of luxury while her family had scraped by on practically nothing.

His father had sent him to Yale. She'd won a scholarship and worked her way through college. She'd paid her way through high school, too, buying her own clothes and supplies.

But life would be different for Rick. He was going to have his chance, no matter what she had to do to secure it.

"Come here," Harrison coaxed in a soft voice.

"What for?"

His assurance that she would do as his bidding caused an unexpected jolt of anger to race over her. She fought a quick battle with her temper while trying to look sassy and only mildly interested in his answer.

She attributed her grumpiness to lack of sleep and the jumpy state of her nerves. After all, she'd never set out on a life of crime before this.

His chuckle preceded him across the room. "Hmm. If the lady won't come to the mountain, the mountain will have to come to the lady. The mountain doesn't mind as long as the end result is the same."

He stopped no more than an inch away. The manly scent of him washed over her. He'd showered before coming down, and he smelled as fresh as a pine tree.

Her throat closed. The air wheezed in and out of her lungs like a rusty accordion. When he braced his hands on the counter on each side of her, she went hot and dizzy.

When she drew a calming breath, balsam aftershave, soap and talc assailed her. If warmth had a scent, that was part of it, too—his male warmth, his bigness, his masculine gentleness.

She inhaled carefully, as if she were a thin crystal container ingesting some potent liquid.

Careful. She had to keep her wits.

"Isa," he murmured.

She heard the need, saw the raw hunger in his eyes.

"Shall we have breakfast?" she asked, not meeting his gaze.

"Isa," he said again. This time it was a growl of demand.

Taking a steadying breath, she gave him her full attention, her expression artfully bland.

Harrison felt a rush of anger when Isa finally met his gaze. Her expression was the same unreadable one he'd seen a hundred times in the past month. It was as intriguing as an unopened package, as frustrating as a misplaced set of keys.

When she looked at him like this—her face so still and composed, her mouth curved into the barest suggestion of a smile—it seemed as if he could see forever in her eyes.

Until he realized a mist whirled and eddied in those green, mysterious depths, obscuring the alluring secrets her enigmatic smile promised she'd reveal to him and him alone.

"Hell," he said.

That startled her. For a second, he thought he saw wariness and some other emotion in those soulful eyes, then it was gone. She smiled brightly at him.

"Curses so early in the morning?" she chided, laughing at his ill-concealed temper.

He leaned over her and inhaled deeply. "You smell good," he murmured. "Like a field of crimson clover. Makes a man think of things...." He nuzzled her ear. "Like early-morning romps." He kissed the corner of her eye. "Like lying in a bed of grass."

She laid her hands, palm down, on his chest. Not in a caress, he noted, but to hold him at bay.

Raising his head, he studied her face, or what he could see of it. She kept it averted from him.

"What is it?" he demanded, puzzled by her attitude. "Are you embarrassed at being here with me?"

"No, of course not."

She held his gaze until he sighed and rested his forehead on hers. Ah, God, the sweetness of it, the mind-boggling delight in holding her, touching her, kissing her....

He abandoned the flight of fancy and brought his mind firmly back to earth. "Believe me, I was as surprised by the fire between us as you were. I can't remember another woman affecting me like that."

For a second, she went utterly still. Her eyes searched his. "How?" she asked. "What do you mean?"

"Well..." He grinned and kissed her upturned nose. "When I think of you, I get all breathless and dizzy. And when I see you, it gets worse. The first time I laid eyes on you, I thought I was going to have a heart attack. Do you think I should see a doctor?" he teased, keeping it light.

In the most subtle of shifts, the mist filled her eyes, obscuring whatever thoughts she might have revealed.

"It doesn't sound too serious. Probably a good night's sleep will take care of it. The coffee is ready."

Before he quite knew how it happened, she'd dipped under the barrier of his arm and removed two mugs from the cabinet. She poured them each some coffee and left his on the counter while she went to the window to gaze out at the lake.

"Clouds are moving in. Do you think it will snow?"

He grabbed the mug and followed her. It came to him that he'd been following her lead all month. Maybe it was time for him to call the shots.

"Maybe." He stopped at her side and sipped the hot brew while trying to decide exactly what shot he wanted to call. "I can't decide what to do about you," he admitted.

"What do you want to do?"

With any other woman, the words would have been provocative. With this one, they were an added layer of confusion. She sounded sincere.

"Take you to bed—"

"That might not be wise," she broke in.

"And keep you there for a month, or two, or three."

Fascinated, he watched a delicate pink tint climb up her neck and into her cheeks. Again, he wished they were alone at the cabin.

"But I have business to attend to," he said. He sounded disgruntled even to himself. Damn, he really was going off the deep end.

"Just think of all that money you're going to make," she reminded him. "I, um, need to go upstairs and dress. I'll just be a minute." She left the kitchen without looking back.

Harrison stood there, watching her until she disappeared up the stairs to the bedroom level. Frowning, he turned back to the glazed, doubled-paned window. If he didn't know better, he'd say she was running from him. The question was...why?

He didn't get a chance to ponder the question. Ken came down to breakfast a few minutes later. He set his controller to scrambling eggs while he stuck a pan of store-bought biscuits in the oven, then started sausage patties cooking.

When Isa returned, this time wearing loafers and jeans with a white turtleneck under a green cable-knit sweater, she set the table in the breakfast nook. They discussed the coming storm while they ate.

He noticed she was all demure composure as she talked to Ken as if they were old buddies. Jealousy was something new to him, but damned if he didn't feel it toward his old friend and college chum, who seemed to put Isa at ease with his corny jokes.

Glancing at his watch, he realized he didn't have time to solve the mystery of Isa Chavez this weekend. But sometime soon, he promised himself, he'd find out what made her tick.

"I'd like to go over those figures one more time," he said to Ken. "We're running a pretty close margin on profit, and I want to make sure we've accounted for every dime."

"Sure."

"I'll do the dishes," Isa volunteered.

"I'll help," Harrison insisted. "You did everything last night."

In the end, they all three worked together. Then Harrison and Ken headed for the study. He was worried about selling off a slice of the mine. It was only twenty percent, but the mine had belonged to his family. He picked up the papers on his desk.

"This is the wrong folder," he said. "What did we do with the contract and those reports?"

"They were here last night." Ken took the papers and shuffled through them. "These are blank pages. Did you put them in a file cabinet or safe?"

"No. They were right here the last time I saw them."

"Would someone take them?" Ken asked, voicing the question that sprang into Harrison's mind.

He shook his head, not in denial, but in puzzlement. "Why? They're not bonds or anything worth money."

"Except to us," Ken reminded him.

Harrison stared at the other man. "Did I put them away? Better question—am I going crazy?" He headed for the wall safe.

"It's probably senility," Ken suggested blandly but with a wiseacre grin.

"Yeah," Harrison agreed. He spun the cylinder. The safe swung open. Its newness was reflected in its emptiness. "Well, that rules out total forgetfulness. Dammit, I know we left those papers on the desk last night, all in a neat pile waiting for signatures."

"Well, that's what I thought—" Ken broke off when Isa appeared in the doorway.

"I may be of help," she said.

Harrison narrowed his eyes and studied her. This time she held his gaze. She wore that beautiful, inscrutable mask that had intrigued him for the past month. He had a feeling he was about to find out what thoughts were hidden behind it.

"Ken," he suggested in a level voice, "why don't you go for a walk?"

Ken glanced from one to the other. "Uh, sure. Be back in, say, an hour?"

"That should be plenty of time," Harrison agreed. Plenty of time for him to wring her neck and find out what she'd done with those reports and the contract that would save the company. He *had* to find it. The deal had to go through.

Isa reminded herself of all the righteous reasons she had for taking those papers. She returned his gaze, refusing to back down in the face of his growing anger.

He stalked toward her, stopping an arm's length away. Choking distance, she thought inanely.

"Where are they?" he asked in a deadly quiet manner.

"In a safe place." She folded her arms across her middle and clutched her elbows as if hanging on to her courage.

"I see." A muscle twitched once in his jaw and was still. He stood without moving, his gaze more puzzled than hostile. "I can call the office and have new copies here within two hours."

"Yes, but you needn't bother. I'll return them—"

He broke in impatiently. "I don't have time for games."

"In plenty of time for your meeting with Mr. Merry." She paused for effect. "After we've reached an agreement."

So far, so good. Her voice was steady and her composure intact, although she had to admit the killer gleam in his eyes was making her a bit nervous.

His lips curved in amusement, surprising her until she realized what it meant. He was contemptuous, mocking her paltry efforts at blackmail.

"We'll see," he said enigmatically and turned on his heel.

She stared at his back, stunned as he walked out. She hadn't prepared for this scenario. She realized where he was going and dashed after him.

He was already halfway up the stairs, taking the steps three at a time in a series of running leaps. She followed his example, but jumped two steps at a time. At the top, she used the newel post to swing into the turn and entered her room only a couple of seconds after Harrison.

She careened into him as she rushed inside. He moved away as if her touch were distasteful. Then he headed for the bed.

With a ruthless thoroughness, he stripped the bed she'd made up an hour ago. With an admirable feat of strength, he tossed the mattress to the floor.

"There's nothing here." She breathed a sigh of relief. The mattress had been the last place she'd selected during the night. It was a good thing she'd moved the papers an hour ago. If he found them, she didn't think he'd listen to her. If he didn't find them, she had a chance to be heard and make her point.

Then he'd probably strangle her.

He methodically went through the entire room, searching every piece of furniture in and out, forward and back. And upside down for good measure.

She was glad she'd moved the nylon bag out of the closet. He'd have found it with no trouble. He checked her apres-ski boots and jacket pockets as well as every shelf.

She waited, arms crossed, for him to finish. "Let me know when you're ready to listen," she said with false patience.

He looked around with a frown, then went to the windows. He searched behind each drape, then checked the outside ledges.

By now, the room looked as if a demolition derby had run through it. Below, she heard the front door open. A draft of cold air swirled over her. Her glance flew to the clock.

"What time are you expecting Mr. Merry?" she asked.

Harrison slammed the last window closed and spun to face her. His expression would have done honor to a death mask.

Her death, she reflected, and suppressed an impulse to burst into hysterical laughter.

"This afternoon around three."

"Five hours," she reminded him.

"I can tell time."

"Fortunately, we don't have far to go or a long wait."

"For what?" He looked big and mean, his fury as cold as an outdoor faucet on a sub-zero morning.

"The wedding."

His chest lifted. His hands clenched into fists. He tossed the mattress back on the bed, then leaned against the dresser, hands in his pockets, legs stretched before him—the epitome of aristocratic hauteur. "Ours, I presume?"

She nodded.

"So that's what this was all about." He gestured around the mussed room. Again he surprised her by smiling. "You were too impatient," he told her.

She watched him warily.

"If you'd waited, you could have had the marriage without this hide-and-seek routine. I was this close to falling in love with you." He lifted a hand and showed her how close.

She felt the pain, a bullet to the heart. She brushed it aside. He was the one playing games, teasing her with a possibility that didn't exist, at least, not for her.

She returned his sardonic smile. "I couldn't take the chance. Love can be…unpredictable." And unreliable. Look at her father. Look at her fiancé.

"You obviously think taking the contract will force me into marriage. Sorry, but I can't see the connection."

"That was to get your attention."

"You got it."

She chose to ignore the sarcasm. She cleared her throat and tried to remember the explanation she'd planned weeks ago. "I have to be married within a month—"

His harsh expletive startled her. His gaze jerked to her abdomen. Heat rushed to her face as she realized how he'd taken her words. "I'm not…I didn't mean…I'm not pregnant," she informed him with great dignity.

He visibly relaxed as if doing it consciously, the way people did in biofeedback clinics.

"No, I didn't really think you were," he said. "You're too sharp to try to trap a man that way in this age of DNA testing."

He let the thought spin into a calculated silence. She realized he was probing, searching for answers or for weak links in her armor. She wouldn't let him find any.

"I did think of it," she confessed with a rush of honesty. "But there wasn't time."

He considered that. "Right. You only have a month." He gave her an impatient glance. "So go on."

She smiled—mysteriously, she hoped—and refused to let him take charge. "Your time is up today. There're only four hours and forty-five minutes left."

He didn't respond. Silence stretched to the breaking point.

"You planned it, didn't you?" he finally said as if seeing the light and not liking what he saw. "Every last detail."

She thought of the hours in his arms. That had been a mistake. Loving made a woman soft and yielding. She had to be ruthless.

"Not every detail, no. I didn't realize how strong..." She stopped, not wanting to give that much to him.

"The passion would be?" he suggested. "That, I admit, was pretty incredible. You should have mentioned marriage night before last. I might have agreed."

"But you might not."

"What makes you think I'll respond any better to blackmail than to passion?"

"You have too much to lose." She was pretty sure she knew him well after a month of observation. Noblesse oblige, family honor and all that, he had it in spades.

"Why me?" he demanded. "You were engaged once. Surely there were other men you could have sunk your hooks into."

Isa flinched inwardly at his choice of words. "You owe us. Your family owes my family." She held his gimlet-eyed gaze with an effort.

"How do you figure that?" His lazy drawl and easy smile belied the controlled fury in the depths of his eyes.

"Your father and mine started the mining business together. My father was cheated out of his share...by yours—"

"The hell you say!"

Harrison was in her face before she could do more than take one step back from his threatening stance.

"My father was one of the most honorable men I ever knew," he told her, his big body looming over hers, his fists propped on his hips in outright menace. "And he never had a partner."

"I have the original document that proves my father was half owner of the mine."

"Let's see it."

"It's in a safety-deposit box." She raised her chin. "Where no one can get hold of it and destroy it. However, I do have a copy with me. I thought you'd insist on seeing it." She dug into her pocket and handed the photocopy over.

She watched in fascination when he glanced at the claim, drew a deep breath and reasserted control over his temper. "How did my father pull this brilliant scam off?"

"A crooked poker game."

Harrison looked as if he might explode. Again he controlled his fury. "I see." He backed up a step and crossed his arms, gesturing with the evidence she'd given him. "So why don't you sue to get your claim reinstated? You'd get half the mine without having to put up with marriage, if this is worth the paper it's written on."

He watched her like a snake eyeing a rabbit. His stare was so intent, she was almost hypnotized by it. "I thought of that when I found the signed claim in my father's papers after he died, but there was no money for lawyers and experts."

When she'd broached the subject to her father a few times after he'd ranted about the loss and the crooked poker game, he'd told her she was stupid, that people like them wielded no power. Who would believe his word over his former partner's?

It wasn't until she came up against the juvenile judge that she'd understood what he meant. No matter what she said or did, the man wouldn't let her have Rick until she was married and could provide a "stable" home.

That attitude smacked of sexism, but she'd had the sense not to say so. Instead she'd devised a plan to claim hers and Rick's rightful inheritance and get the home they had to have.

"I have a legitimate claim on the mine," she continued. "That paper proves it. Unless you agree to marriage, I'll show your investor my claim and tell him I intend to get a restraining order on any deal you sign."

Harrison didn't speak. He simply watched her as if she were an interesting specimen at a zoo. It made her uneasy.

"There's one more thing," she said.

"Now why did I suspect there might be?" he murmured.

She steeled herself to put on a brave front. This might be the hardest part. "My brother...Rick..."

Harrison looked mildly surprised when she brought up the subject of her brother. "Yes?" he snapped.

"He has to live with us."

Silence greeted her rushed statement. Finally Harrison gave her a feral smile. "Anything else?"

"You have to go with me to get him."

"Where is he?"

"In Oregon."

Harrison leaned an elbow on the back of a chair and stroked his chin as if studying the situation. "When?" he asked.

"In a month."

When he didn't speak but continued to look at her with his dark brows slightly raised, she explained rapidly, "He's to be turned over to court-appointed guardians at that time, either the state or...or me, if I can provide a home."

"Ah." A light dawned in his eyes. She wondered how much he really understood. If he knew how hard it was to face him, how frightened she was for her brother, how desperate...

She locked her hands together. "It will be a marriage in name only, but to the world we must present a picture of marital bliss. For the judge and the social worker."

"I see. You get a home for yourself and your brother from the marriage. What do I get?"

She had the answer. "An annulment. In one year, the parole period will be up. Then, as soon as Rick gets out of school next June, we can file for an annulment."

He gave a snort of laughter, whether in amusement or not, she couldn't tell. He read over the claim signed by his father and hers once more.

"It's genuine," she insisted.

Without acknowledging her statement, he went to the phone and punched in a number. In less than a minute, he was speaking to his attorney. She clutched her arms across her middle and waited while Harrison read every word on the claim into the receiver. After a five-minute discussion with the lawyer, Harrison demanded, "Just tell me if it could be real."

He listened, said a succinct curse, then hung up. He turned to her, his eyes like two glacier chips. "Even if this is upheld in court, you won't be getting much. The mining company is running on a shoestring. It hasn't made a profit in years."

She nodded. She knew his troubles in detail. As a business major in college, she knew how to find information.

"People will lose their jobs, their homes, if you force me to close the mine," he added. "The jewelry-making business isn't enough to carry the operation or pay off the money my father had to borrow to stay in business."

She watched him warily. She knew about that, too. The E.P.A. had forced the company to invest heavily in new equipment for pollution control. It was only because she knew he was over a financial barrel that she'd dared this form of blackmail. He had to have Merry's money; she had to have a home.

"If I'm to be married, I'm going to get all the benefits that go with it." His gaze roamed her entire body from head to foot, with several pauses along the way, and back again.

She gasped aloud. It hadn't occurred to her that he would want to have anything to do with her, other than keeping up the remotest facade to fool the judge and social worker. "No—"

"But yes," he interrupted. "That sample you allowed me Saturday only whetted my appetite for more. Marriage might not be so bad if I can look forward to you in my bed every night."

"No, I...we can't." That wasn't in her plan.

"A celibate year? Is that what you're suggesting?" His eyes glowed like hot coals. "No way."

She collected her poise with an effort. "I won't cause problems or interfere in your life. If you must have companions, I won't object...as long as you're discreet."

"Very noble of you," he murmured. "So I'm to have complete freedom in this marriage farce?"

He pushed away from the dresser and came to her. She stayed where she was, even when he stood almost toe to toe with her.

"You should have used your powers of persuasion to talk me into marriage," he murmured in the softest of loverlike purrs. "Maybe you should try them now. I've forgotten what I'll get in the matrimonial package. Refresh my memory."

His breath caressed her face as he bent close enough to allow her to demonstrate her lovemaking techniques on him.

"If your memory fails, use your imagination."

"No, we'll do it your way. Remember what happened when we kissed? Your lips trembled...yes, like that...just a little...as if it were your first time...."

He lowered his head to hers as he spoke. With the last word, his mouth touched hers. Then he waited.

His tactics were blatantly unfair. It was all she could do not to melt against him. A woman could find peace and safety in those arms. If he offered them. At the very least she might drown in his eyes. He was so close she could see the golden lines that connected the brown centers to the blue outer edges.

Isa blinked and prayed for the strength to play this tease-and-tempt game with him. She was suddenly afraid he was more ruthless than she could ever be.

The ringing of the telephone didn't make him back off.

How long they would have stayed there, their lips lightly touching as he waited for her to make a move, she didn't know. Ken came to her rescue.

"Uh, Harrison, that was Zeke Merry. His plane will land in about an hour. He wants to meet for lunch before coming back here to go over the agreement."

Harrison moved fractionally apart from her. "Thanks. I'll see you in the study in a few minutes."

"Right."

Isa heard Ken's retreating footsteps on the stairs. She maintained her Brigitte Bardot expression, but inside she felt equal parts relief and apprehension.

"I don't like the idea of living a lie," he announced. It sounded as if he was turning her down.

"The contract with Mr. Merry," she reminded him. A sense of desolation swept over her. She couldn't fail. She'd worked so hard to accomplish this plan. "You can't sell off part of the company without my approval. I won't give it."

"Yes, there is that. Well, the company will go under, but what the hell? I'll still have the jewelry-making business. The families that depend on the mine for their living will have to take care of themselves."

This wasn't going at all the way she'd planned. She rubbed her forehead and tried to think.

He took a step toward the door. "Marriage my way or not at all. Which will it be?"

"You can't possibly want to...to..."

"You have no idea what I want," he told her, his tone so soft it frightened her. "I didn't plan on inheriting a failing silver mine when my father died last year, but that's what I got. I didn't plan on a forced marriage, but it looks like that's what I'll have to take." He looked at his watch. "Make up your mind, sweetheart. Time, as the poets like to say, is a-flying."

His smile was hard, but he wouldn't hurt her, not in any physical sense. He might make life miserable for a year, but it hadn't been wonderful in ages, so that didn't matter.

"Okay," she agreed.

"To everything?"

Her throat closed. She nodded.

"Then hurry. You have five minutes to prepare for a wedding." After giving her one more cutting glance, he went down the stairs, presumably heading for the library to inform Ken of the change in plans.

Isa fell back against the door. *Married.* He'd agreed. They were getting *married.*

She clutched both hands against her chest. Only one thought came to mind. *Out of the frying pan and into the fire.*

The bong of a clock somewhere in the house reminded her of time's passage. She leapt over the crumpled sheets on the floor—heavens, what had Ken thought upon seeing the bedroom in a mess and Harrison and her standing lip-to-lip, without moving?

Looking through her mussed clothing, she realized there was one thing she hadn't thought of during her mad scheming. She hadn't bought a wedding dress.

Chapter Four

The wedding chapel was next to the lake.

"You may choose whichever view you prefer," the justice of the peace, an older man who was hastily slipping into a suit jacket, told Isa. This decision was clearly within the purview of the bride in his estimation.

The chapel was on the upper level of the building. One plate-glass window framed a picture-perfect scene of Lake Tahoe with snowy mountain peaks in the distance. The window in the adjacent wall gave a view of lofty mountains covered in snow-crested evergreens perched against a backdrop of sapphire sky. A bit of lake was visible in the right corner of the window.

The justice's wife smiled benignly from the bench in front of an electronic organ. Live music was twenty-five dollars extra, she explained, looking their clothing over to ferret out a clue to how much money they might spend. "Shall I play for you?"

"Oh, yes, by all means, let's shoot the works," Harrison agreed before Isa could refuse.

The plump wife perked right up at Harrison's sardonic remark. The next thing Isa knew a bridal nosegay of pink sweetheart roses and white baby's breath was thrust into her hand. Only fifty dollars.

Harrison bought it. The matronly woman looked regretfully at Harrison and Ken's casual clothing and the boutonnieres in the handy refrigerated display case.

Isa had chosen her black slacks and white silk blouse with the gold belt and earrings for her wedding outfit. The two men were in jeans and shirts with sweaters.

"We have wedding rings," the wife said, "in case you haven't had time to shop for them."

"This was rather a sudden decision, wasn't it, darling?" Harrison gave her a squeeze and a wink that had her gritting her teeth to keep from telling him to pack it in. "Yes, let's look at the rings."

When he'd picked one for her from a large selection in a jeweler's case, she chose one for him, too.

"Look," she said, pointing out the discreet sign. "The second ring is half price when you buy two at the same time."

"Wonderful, darling," he agreed warmly. "I want the world to know I'm a married man."

She nearly choked at the tender look he gave her. Ken looked amazed. In fact, he'd worn a bemused expression all morning, as if wondering if he was going to wake up soon. She could identify with the feeling.

Harrison was the epitome of the happy-go-lucky groom. And she was certainly the nervous bride. The nosegay shook like a field of wildflowers in a gale. In her left hand, she clutched the wedding band for her groom.

"Don't be nervous, darling," Harrison leaned close

to say. "I'll make a marvelous husband—tender and sensitive and all the things you modern women want."

The justice's wife nearly swooned at his feet. Isa gave the woman a heated glare, then turned it on her groom, who gave her an innocent-as-a-shorn-lamb smile.

She wasn't sure who was getting fleeced here.

"We have champagne, already chilled," the wife sang out, bustling around the chapel and setting out the extra flower baskets…only two hundred dollars.

"We don't have time," Harrison said with a world of regret in his richly melodic voice.

There was also no time for Isa to further protest the unnecessary expenses. The justice picked up his little black book and opened it. He cleared his throat loudly.

Isa faced the lake and kept her eyes riveted on the far mountains as he began the ceremony in a rumbling monotone.

This was only for a year. She could stand anything for a year. During the ritual, she repeated the words of wisdom that had gotten her this far in her scheme.

There was nothing Harrison could do in a year that would make her give up, she vowed. One year, then she and Rick could move to some small town where no one would know them and start their lives over with a clean slate.

"I do," she answered almost gaily when the justice paused in his reading and looked at her.

"I do faithfully promise," the justice repeated.

She hadn't realized she was supposed to repeat the vows. "I do faithfully pr—" The word snagged in her throat. She swallowed hard. This wasn't a real promise, she reminded herself. "I do faithfully promise…."

Harrison repeated his vows without a hitch.

"I now pronounce you man and wife," the justice intoned.

"Good," Harrison said grimly, all signs of his feigned cheer gone. He glanced at his watch. "Let's get out of here. The plane will be landing in fifteen minutes."

"But wait," the justice cried.

Three sets of eyes glared at him.

"You...ah...forgot to kiss the bride."

A beat of silence passed, then Harrison turned toward her. "So I did," he said. He grabbed her wrist and reeled her in like a fish on the end of a line.

For a second, she resisted. Then, at the narrowing of his eyes, she realized what she was doing. Foregoing the useless struggle, she assumed a radiant smile. "Oh, yes, darling, the kiss," she murmured and pulled his head down to hers.

Somehow he kept turning the tables on her and gaining the upper hand. If she was going to endure, she had to take control. She would show him he couldn't manhandle her. She plastered herself aggressively to him.

Her lips tingled at the first touch, then sizzled as his mouth covered hers. He gave her a lover's kiss that burned clear down to her toes. She couldn't breathe...or think....

His tongue stroked her lips, then delved inside as she opened to him, unable to stop the response. His hands roamed her back but stayed respectfully above her waist.

An uncontrollable tremor raced through her.

For a second his arms tightened convulsively, then he released her. She swayed dizzily. He held her shoulders until she regained her balance. Confused, she could only stare up at him, not sure what had happened in those few seconds.

A shower of flower petals hit her in the face. The plump wife tossed them into the air and romped around like one of those nymphs dressed in billowy veils that appeared in old paintings Isa had seen in museums. Ken and the justice were smiling broadly.

"Now let's get the documents signed," the justice suggested.

With a shaky scrawl, Isa signed her name to the marriage certificate that would be registered with the State of Nevada that very day.

"Let's go," her groom said, a grim expression in his eyes, taking charge once more.

Harrison drove them to the airport, Ken in the back seat and Isa in the front. She clenched her hands together. The unfamiliar gold circle on her third finger, left hand, bit into her flesh. She stared at the ring as if she'd never seen one before.

Married. He'd probably strangle her before the year was up. Especially when she made one more demand of him—to continue his act as the loving groom until the judge released her brother into her care.

They arrived at the tiny airport only minutes before the private plane set down on the tarmac. Two men climbed out—the pilot, a man in his thirties, she estimated, and... "He is an old codger," she said, surprised into speaking.

Zeke Merry looked like a prospector just returning to civilization after months in the desert. He wore old boots, baggy jeans, a frayed shirt and a sheepskin jacket that should have been put out to pasture years ago.

"Don't let his looks fool you," Ken told her. "He's as cagey as they come. And a stickler for high morals. He wouldn't have approved of you being at the cabin alone with Harrison."

She wondered if the old man would approve of their rushed marriage. Harrison introduced Ken to the tycoon, then looped an arm around her waist. "And this is Isa." He gave a hard-edged smile. "My wife."

The watery blue eyes in the wrinkled parchment face zoomed in on her. Isa smiled pleasantly and squirmed under the intent regard of the old man.

Or was it the feel of Harrison's fingers lightly caressing her along her waist that had her suddenly restless?

"Wife, eh? I don't recall you being married," Zeke stated.

"It was fairly recent," Harrison inserted smoothly. "We're still on our honeymoon."

Isa stared in stunned surprise as the old codger clouded up. Tears actually formed in his eyes.

"I'm glad to hear it. Marriage steadies a fellow," he said, nodding his head wisely. "A man oughtn't to be alone. I still miss my Abby and she's been gone fifteen years or more."

Isa guessed his age to be in the seventies or eighties. It was hard to tell. He was one of those people who looked as if he'd been born old and time hadn't improved his looks.

"I'm glad to meet you," she said politely, and held out a hand.

He grabbed her hand and pulled her close enough to buss her on the cheek and offer some advice. "You keep that man of yours in line. Women got more sense than men any day of the week."

"My sentiments exactly." Isa glanced at Harrison. "You didn't tell me Mr. Merry was a philosopher, darling, and a brilliant one at that."

"Call me Zeke." He pulled out an old-fashioned pocket watch. "It's nigh past my lunch hour, and my stomach's rattling like a set of bones in a cup. Where can we eat around here?"

"I've made reservations. Is your pilot joining us?"

"No, thanks, I'm going to check out the plane," the pilot said. "There's a hum I don't like." He nodded and left them.

"Cole don't cotton much to people," Zeke said sadly as if this was a personal loss.

"What happened to him?" Isa asked. She watched the pilot's solitary figure head for the greasy-spoon restaurant in the airport. He had the aura of a loner who trusted few people.

"His daddy was killed when he was a tyke, then his ma lit out with another man when he was fourteen."

"Did she leave him with relatives?"

"Nah, she left him on his own."

Isa's heart went out to the man. She'd been so worried about holding the family together and raising her brother when her mother had died. It had been an enormous responsibility.

"Our reservations are for one," Harrison broke in. His arm tightened around her, pulling her solidly against him.

When she glanced up in question, she saw a glitter of emotion in his eyes, then it was gone. She tried to figure out what it had been. She knew he was still angry with her over the marriage, but this had been directed at the pilot.

Could it have been...? No, surely not. Harrison wouldn't be jealous, especially not of her.

Zeke insisted she ride in front with her new husband. He rode in the back with Ken and talked nonstop about the changes in the area since he'd last been there. "Back a few years, it was," he reminisced over a lunch of barbecued spareribs. "I came to visit a widow, but it didn't work out. Her kids didn't approve."

Isa licked the sauce off her fingers. This was her wedding luncheon, she realized. She nearly laughed. Her best friend, who lived in California now, would appreciate the irony.

They had decided as teenagers to marry rich men, have beautiful children and live next door to each other. Neither of them had gotten all three wishes, although Carly seemed happy with her tall, silent rancher and his son.

While the men talked of world affairs, then the baseball season, her thoughts remained stubbornly rooted in the dreams she'd once had. Nine years ago, nothing had seemed impossible; now everything did....

Harrison laid a penny beside her plate.

She felt her color rise as she glanced around the table. The three men were watching her with various expressions on their faces. Zeke acted the irascible old man, but his eyes were kind.

Ken was worried, probably about the future of the company.

Isa turned to her husband. His expression was amused, but his eyes still smoldered. It would take only a spark to rekindle his earlier fury at being tricked into marriage.

He laid another penny beside the first.

Put on the spot, she had to say something. "I was thinking of children...of my brother," she amended. "I'll be glad to see him again."

"Where is he?" Zeke asked.

"He's at a juvenile detention center in Oregon." She might as well tell the whole of it. Harrison would find out soon enough. "He was arrested in connection with a warehouse theft."

"You ought to take a broomstick to him," was Zeke's advice.

She locked her hands together in her lap, remembering the past. "My father used his belt. It only made Rick more determined to defy him."

"Did he use it on you, too?" Harrison asked in a peculiar tone of voice. His eyes glittered with emotions she couldn't define.

"No." She smiled defiantly. "I learned early not to talk back. Men don't like to be told what they're doing wrong."

"Especially by their women." Harrison laid his hand over hers. He rubbed her knuckles until she relaxed her grip. When she moved her hands apart, he took his hand away. "Ready to go?"

She nodded.

They left the restaurant and returned to the mountain house. Zeke was assigned to the bedroom with the private bath, the one that had been hers.

Staring at the closed door after the old man had disappeared inside, she wondered what the night would bring. Would Harrison really expect all the rights of marriage?

Tingles rushed over her. Her heart pounded very fast. To her dismay, she couldn't decide if her nervous qualms were from fear or anticipation.

"See you in the study in half an hour," he said to Ken.

Ken nodded and went into his room. The door closed behind him without a sound. All Isa could hear was the rapid beat of her heart.

"I had your things moved to my room while we were gone," Harrison explained with a casual wave of his hand toward the closed door. "My neighbor," he added by way of explanation.

"The one who takes care of things for you?"

"Yeah. I asked her to come over and make up the guest room. She tidied up the place, too."

"I think—"

"We'll talk later. There isn't time now."

Harrison took her arm and ushered her across the sky bridge and into the master bedroom. He gave the door a shove, a much gentler one than he would have liked. It closed with a smooth click of the latch behind them.

His bride faced him with that artfully blank expression. If she was scared of him and the consequences of her acts, she wasn't showing it.

A hint of admiration warred with the anger that gripped him. Yeah, she had courage. He'd concede that. Too bad she was a lying, conniving witch to go with it.

Forget it. This wasn't the time to hash over the virtues of his newly acquired wife. He had more urgent problems.

"Right now I need those reports and the contract. How soon can you produce them?"

She walked over to the king-size bed and reached under the mattress. She withdrew the documents and handed them to him with a little flourish.

"I have to hand it to you—you have talent and imagination," he murmured. "Intelligence, too. I'd never have thought of looking there."

"That's what I counted on."

"But then, blackmail was far from my mind at the time," he continued as if she hadn't spoken.

She had the grace to turn away. He watched her walk to the French doors leading to the hot tub. Tall and lithe, she walked like a jungle cat on the prowl.

Yeah, and he was the hunk of meat she'd caught.

He shuffled through the papers. All there. "I've arranged for dinner to be catered at seven. We should be through with the meeting by five. Can you entertain yourself until then?"

"Yes."

He reached for the door, then paused with his hand on the knob. "I'll need to know everything and everyone involved in your brother's case. If you'll write it down, I'll give the info to my attorney and have him see what he can do when we get back to Reno tomorrow."

"I...thank-you," she said softly.

She didn't turn to him. A sudden need to see her expression made him cross the room. When he stopped beside her, he still wasn't sure what he was going to do.

Her gaze slid up to his, then away.

He clasped her chin and held her face up to his. Then, slowly and deliberately, he bent and kissed her. Her mouth formed a perfect rosebud of surprise.

"That will have to hold me until later," he said, and left the room before he made a bigger fool of himself.

He wasn't sure what he was going to do about his marriage or his bride, but lingering in a bedroom wasn't the best place for clearheaded thinking about it.

Isa changed her silk blouse for a warm sweater before going down to dinner. The temperature had dropped as the clouds moved in and hovered over the Tahoe basin.

"Snow before morning," Zeke predicted as they lingered over brandy and coffee in the study. "Will the plane be able to get out of the airport?"

"Probably not. The passes will be closed, too. We might have to stay an extra day." Harrison glanced at Isa.

She curled deeper into the recliner, thinking of being snowed in with him. Except her musings didn't run to two other people being present. If only...

No, she couldn't afford to think like that. She had to

live in the real world. And that included the night ahead of them.

A lump of apprehension formed in her throat. She sipped the brandy, letting its warmth dissolve her fears. She took another drink, then another. Ken refilled her glass.

"Thank you." She smiled at him, her one possible friend in this house. She raised the glass to her lips, saw her husband scowling at her from across the room, and lifted the snifter in a mock toast. His eyes never left hers as he toasted her and drank at the same time she did.

Shivers ran over her. She was cold inside. Outside, too. Her hands felt like two blocks of ice. She wished the night was over and done with.

The grandfather clock bonged eleven times.

Harrison came to her and expertly removed the glass from her numb fingers. "Run along to bed, darling. I'll be up in a minute."

He pulled her to her feet and sent her on her way with a pat on her behind. She gave him a fierce glance to let him know she wouldn't be patronized, then smiled graciously at Zeke and Ken.

"Good night," she said gaily. "Don't keep him up too long." She gave Harrison a you-naughty-boy smile.

Zeke chuckled. "Watch out for that little filly, boy," he advised. "I don't think she takes easily to a man's hand."

Harrison's smile was like his drawl—sort of lazy, amused, in control. "She'll learn to take mine."

Isa drew herself up with great dignity. "I'm not a horse to be reined to any man's bidding."

Zeke cackled with merriment. "Just like my Abby, as independent as a fox, but she tamed down gentle enough once we married.'' His laughter faded to a smile that brought a pang to Isa's heart.

With Harrison's hand on her elbow, she strolled to the stairs. He made sure she had hold of the banister before he let her go. Head high, she marched up to them, aware of her husband's gaze burning over her as she ascended.

Crossing the sky bridge, she realized she needed the support of the banister. She was definitely woozy.

She giggled. Tipsy on her wedding night...and scared of her husband. That thought sobered her. She wasn't scared of any man. And she wouldn't be told what to do.

Chin set in determination, she washed up and changed into her long-sleeved, fleecy nightgown. When she turned down the bed and climbed in, she had another rush of apprehension. She quelled it fiercely.

Men were an unreliable lot at best, but neither her father nor her fiancé had frightened her. Neither would her husband.

When she stretched out on the bed, her heart beat very fast, and her mind rushed crystal clear over troubled thoughts.

Harrison entered the dark bedroom more than an hour after his bride had retired. He'd deliberately stayed with the men downstairs. He flipped on the lamp on his side of the bed, not sure what to expect. He wasn't even sure his wife would be here.

She was.

Looking like an angel, she slept deeply, her face beautiful in repose. That artfully controlled expression was gone. In its place was the person she hid from the world.

Her slumber was restless. Under the faint, bluish

tinge on her eyelids, her eyes moved in REM sleep. A frown furrowed her brow.

It came to him that she rarely frowned…and neither did she smile or laugh uninhibitedly. Control. She was always under the watchful eye of self-control.

But then, con artists had to be careful not to give themselves away before they played their hand, he reminded himself as the anger surged anew at her angelic appearance.

"You'd make a hell of a poker player, lady," he muttered.

Her eyes opened.

"Sorry," he said. "I didn't mean to wake you."

He noted she awoke instantly, her mind alert and knowing where she was with no confusion. Alarm flashed in her eyes and was instantly gone, replaced by that bland, watchful expression that gave nothing away. He wondered what she'd felt when they'd nearly made love.

"Did you fake it?" he asked her, as if continuing a conversation they'd begun earlier.

His ego wanted to deny that a woman could fool him that completely, but his innate honesty forced him to admit the possibility.

"Fake what?"

"The passion. The way you melted in my arms. The way you touched me. The way you *wanted* me."

He studied her as she blinked up at him, her gaze wary, her thoughts obscured by the veil she kept between her and the world.

"Don't you know?" she finally asked.

He shook his head. "But I will. Before the year is up, I'll figure out what makes you tick. And then…"

Fear raced along Isa's backbone like a mouse scurrying from a cat. She held her breath for an instant, then regained her faltering courage.

There was nothing he could do, not even in a forced marriage, to make her run.

As he leaned over her without speaking, she found herself trapped in his gaze. Her thinking processes faltered, then halted. While not movie-star handsome, her husband was incredibly attractive in her eyes.

He had a broad, high forehead with a stubborn wave of dark hair falling across it. His eyebrows were dark and thick. When he grew old, they would become bushy and rather formidable. She would trim them for him so he wouldn't scare the grandchildren—

"What?" he asked, as if sensing her troubled thoughts.

She shook her head. His grandchildren wouldn't be hers.

Freeing one hand from the covers, she brushed the shiny lock of hair from his forehead. His face was sculpted in hard angles that flowed into the flat planes of his cheekbones. The set of his chin indicated a firm will, that of his mouth a wry sense of humor. All in all, it was a face filled with intelligence and resolve, a face that could be trusted....

She dropped her hand to the sheet, feeling herself dangerously close to being feminine and foolish.

He caught her hand and laid it on his chest. "Touch me," he ordered in a soft voice that was almost a caress. "It's the one thing between us that's right."

She pulled free. "I can't believe you'd want me to after...after today's events."

For another ten seconds, he stared at her without a word. "So it was all a pretense," he said, the cold fury returning. He got up from the edge of the bed and walked out.

Isa waited, her body tense, her senses alert for his return. She waited for hours. He didn't come back that night.

Chapter Five

"How long will this snow keep up?" Zeke asked. He paced to the broad window and watched the huge, feathery flakes tumble from a bed of clouds.

"According to the weather station, it's supposed to start clearing by noon," Ken reported.

The crusty tycoon trudged back to the hearth, where Harrison had built a fire right after breakfast. "How about a game of poker? Anyone want to take me on?"

No one answered.

"I will," Isa decided, laying the magazine aside. She wondered if Harrison had spent the night in the study. If so, there had been no sign of it this morning.

"Cards are in one of the drawers," Harrison told them, pointing to a game table at the back of the room.

She and Zeke moved over to the table. They checked the side drawers. Isa found the playing cards. She removed them from the box, shuffled, then fanned them three times and slid them over to Zeke to cut.

"Name your poison," she invited. "Five-card draw? Seven-card stud? One-eyed jacks wild?"

Zeke flicked her a calculating grin. "You name it, little girl. I want to see your game."

"I only play for matches." She swept the cut deck toward her and readied one card. "Anyone else want in?"

"I'll be the bank," Harrison decided. He removed stacks of colorful chips from another drawer and counted out an even number for each player.

"I'll pass," Ken said, nose buried in a report.

With expert skill, Isa dealt the cards and put the rest of the deck aside. Zeke tossed an ante chip in the middle of the table. She did likewise. He beat her four hands straight.

Then she really began to play.

She took three hands, then he hit a flush. She folded and let him take the pot.

"Dang it, girl, why didn't you at least call?"

"I couldn't beat you."

"You didn't have anything?" He reached for the cards she'd tossed facedown on the felt and flipped them over. "A pair of jacks. You had a pair of jacks and didn't bet them?"

Isa gathered the cards and fanned them into each other. When she looked up, she spoke in a menacing drawl like a gunslinger in a B Western. "Where I come from, mister, a man could lose a hand for less than that."

All three men looked suitably startled by her reminder of the rules. She smiled coolly and dealt the cards.

Three hours later, the hallway clock bonged noon. Isa had a big stack of chips in front of her. Zeke had five left. He shoved them into the middle.

"Last hand," he said. "Winner take all."

She laughed softly and slid all her chips forward. Her opponent tossed three cards down and took three. She discarded two and drew two.

"Okay, girl, let's see what's making you so happy," he barked at her, sounding like a wheezy old guard dog.

By now, Ken and Harrison were both engrossed in the play of the two experts. In spite of Isa's steady wins, it was obvious that Zeke was no greenhorn at the game.

She spread out the five cards. "Ace-high straight."

Zeke threw his cards down with an irritated whack. "You've been reading me since the fourth hand. What did I do to give myself away? What'd I do?" he demanded of Harrison when she wouldn't tell him.

Harrison considered, then shrugged. "Sometimes you draw the cards closer when you have a good hand."

Zeke gave a disgruntled snort. "Is that it?"

"That's one thing."

"You mean there's more?"

Isa nodded in the face of his disbelieving scowl. "Your lips are softer when you have a good hand, harder when you don't." She put the cards away. "Look, the sun is breaking through the clouds. I'll prepare lunch, then maybe we can go."

She left the men in the study, Zeke still growling about his loss and arguing whether he gave his hands away or not.

"Lips! Who can tell anything about lips? They're on a person's face. Hard, soft, so what? Who can tell whether lips are hard or soft?"

"Isa can," Harrison said, following Isa into the kitchen. "So can I," he murmured to himself.

His bride barely looked his way before she began

putting together ham-and-cheese sandwiches. She used the last of the kosher dill pickles from the jar and sliced the last apple as a side dish.

"That was impressive playing. You could take it up as a living," he suggested.

"No, thanks. Life is precarious enough."

He stuck his hands in his back pockets to keep from reaching for her, to stop her busy hands from touching anything but him. "Where did you learn?"

He probed for information, curiosity eating at him. Well, hell, a man ought to know something about his wife.

She piled the sandwiches on a platter. "I used to play against my father."

"He must have been one hell of a player."

"Why do you assume he was the better player?" She removed plates and mugs from the cupboard, then found a tray under the cabinet. "Sometimes it takes more skill to lose."

"Ah," he said. She'd learned early to conceal her abilities. He wondered what else she hid behind that smile that disclosed so little about her inner thoughts.

He found himself in danger of being fascinated all over again by the woman he'd married so precipitously. He wanted to know who the real woman was—the one who'd come apart in his hands and responded so beautifully to him that it still stopped his breath, or this cool poker player who shuffled the deck with easy skill and asked for no quarter.

The anger surged anew. He had a year. By damn, he would know her inside and out before twelve months had gone by.

With this thought in mind, he went to her. She was stacking sandwich plates on the tray. When he slipped his arms around her, she tensed, but wasn't startled. She'd known he was near.

Good. He wanted her aware of his presence at all times.

"I missed you last night," he murmured, nuzzling along her neck. He inhaled the warm, womanly scent of her. The blood rushed from his head to his groin in a dizzy sweep. It was enough to make a man forget what he was about.

"Where did you sleep?"

She immediately pressed her lips closed. He chuckled. "Curious?"

"Not particularly. I just wondered."

"On the sofa in the study with only a blanket and memories to keep me warm."

He grinned when she gave a little unladylike snort at his bid for sympathy. He let his hands wander away from her waist. With his left one, he explored the gentle slope of her abdomen, letting the very tips of his fingers drift over the womanly mound.

She caught her breath, then exhaled slowly.

Letting his right hand glide upward, he paused below the tempting thrust of her breast. She stopped loading the tray.

He leaned into her, letting her feel the strength of his desire. A spark of triumph went through him when she trembled.

However, passion was a two-edged sword. He, too, was caught in the sensual snare he'd set, his body aching.

"Look at me," he demanded.

She tilted her head and looked over her shoulder at him. He brushed her mouth with his. A groan worked its way out of him.

"A taste isn't enough," he whispered against her lips.

He turned her without breaking the contact, needing the feel of her against him, breast to breast, thigh to thigh. Bending, he lifted her so that his erection snuggled against the sweet indentation at the joining of her legs.

She drew back with a little sound of alarm. He reached up and cupped her face in his hand, holding her like a golden chalice, while he sipped the nectar from her lips. He kissed her until she stopped resisting and responded.

He broke the kiss with a muttered curse and pressed his face into the dark cloud of hair that fell about her shoulders. "My God," he said, shaken right to the marrow of his bones.

"Please." She pushed against him, but her hands felt like butterflies fluttering over him, luring him deeper into the sensuous spell.

"Say, Harrison...uh, never mind."

Harrison lifted his head and glanced around. Ken was beating a hasty retreat for the kitchen door.

"It's okay," he said in a forced drawl, feeling like the biggest of fools for having been caught kissing his wife in the middle of the day. His anger extended to himself, as he let Isa go.

Ken stopped at the door. "Zeke called the airport. His plane will be ready to go in an hour. The summit road is clear, too. I thought I'd head back if you don't need me."

Harrison cleared the huskiness of desire from his throat. "Yeah, it's time we were getting on in, too. Isa has lunch ready. We'll take off as soon as we eat."

"Right. Shall I bring the tray?" Ken asked his hostess, his eyes raking her over as if looking for wounds.

"Yes, please," Isa answered. She reached for mugs and poured fresh coffee in them, then placed them on another tray along with spoons, the cream pitcher and a bowl of sugar.

Harrison was pleased to see her hands were shaky...just as his were. Getting lost in passion hadn't been his plan, he reminded himself savagely. He'd wanted to test her a bit, to find out if her response had been faked or the real thing.

He'd learned one thing—his own was overwhelmingly real.

Isa stared listlessly at the road. A cold wind buffeted Harrison's luxury sedan. Snow covered the sides of the hills and outlined each tree as they dropped over the summit and down into Eagle Valley. A panorama view of the desert opened before them.

The storm hadn't reached this far. The exposed earth was dun colored. The clumps of sage were gray-green. When they descended to the floor of the arid valley, she looked back at the mountains. They seemed unreal.

Everything about the weekend seemed a dream. She glanced at her husband, lost in his own thoughts...grim ones, she was willing to bet. The weekend probably seemed like a nightmare to him. And it wasn't over yet.

She sighed and faced the road leading to Reno. Now that she'd accomplished her goal, she was nervous and on edge. She didn't know what Harrison was going to expect or demand from her. She hated being unsure.

Her life since her mother had died had been one uncertainty after another as she'd taken over most of the responsibility for her small family. She'd worked after school to make ends meet. That hadn't left much time for dating. Until her last year of college, she'd never had a boyfriend.

Glancing at the stern profile of her new husband, she realized she had very little experience with men outside her own family circle. Her brief fling at a relationship had been a heady spring romance, more sparkle than true fire. Harrison was different, a man, not a boy, and not one who could be fooled by her silences and purposely blank expression.

"I'll be tied up in meetings while we get the new contract under way. Sometimes I work all night at the office."

She nodded in understanding.

"You won't mind, will you?"

"No, of course not."

"Of course not," he repeated.

She couldn't read anything unusual in his tone, but a chill danced along her nerves as if he'd spoken in a threatening voice.

"As long as you get the semblance of a marriage, enough to fool the judge, that's all you care about, right?"

"Yes." She wasn't going to let him goad her into a fight if that was what he was after.

"I can have all the women I want...discreetly, I believe you said?"

She clenched her hands, stopping an instinctive protest by dint of will. "Yes."

That was the bargain. She could stand it for a year.

"You know, I think this might work. I've heard that the best marriages are those based on friendship rather than something so fickle and elusive as love. We can be great friends, give your brother the stable home he needs and enjoy the freedom of an open marriage."

He sounded so smugly pleased as he counted the advantages of their marriage that she wanted to hit him. She bit the inside of her lip and said nothing.

"Of course, there are those who think marriage is a sacred commitment. But we have an agreement, a business contract, as it were. Isn't that right?"

"Why ask me?" she said at last, feeling compelled to respond to the one-sided conversation. "You have it all figured out."

"Do I?" he questioned on a harsher note. "I wonder."

She was glad when he fell silent for the rest of the ride. Behind them, Ken followed at a safe distance in a four-wheel-drive vehicle. She wished she could have ridden with him, but she suspected Harrison would never have allowed it.

Harrison drove directly to his family home, which was nestled in a dip on top of a hill overlooking the city. She hadn't yet been inside the wood-and-stone structure. She'd been too busy at the center. He'd had to come to her that month.

Her mouth was totally dry by the time he parked in the three-car garage. A red sports car occupied one spot.

"Welcome home," her husband said with a cynical smile as he threw the side door open on its well-oiled hinges.

The foyer was an atrium, from which the sky was visible through domed panels of glass. The interior of the house was guarded by a wall of black wrought-iron fencing. Harrison went to a concealed pad and punched in a code. The gate swung open.

"Very impressive," she murmured when he looked at her.

Again she had the impression of a young man showing off a treasure the same way he'd done at the mountain retreat. It was confusing. He surely didn't give a damn what she thought about his living arrangements.

"Maggie Bird is the housekeeper. She comes in during the week. She leaves meals in the refrigerator for dinner. If you don't like those arrangements, work it out with her.''

"That sounds fine." She meant to have as little impact on his life as possible during their year. That was only fair. No disruption, no scenes, no jealous rages over his women. If she was lucky, she'd never know about them.

"This way," he said, crossing a marble-tiled hall.

To her left was a lovely living room done in desert colors of dun and dark, brick-toned red. Turquoise and silver jewelry was displayed on one wall in enclosed frames, as if they were pictures.

A den with a huge television was behind the living room. The study and kitchen were on the right. Beyond the kitchen, doors opened onto the patio, which was lined with trees and shrubs in huge pots, making an oasis of the place.

"The master suite," Harrison announced, leading the way across another atrium filled with wicker furniture and views of the mountains on one side and the valley on the other. He opened the door and stepped inside.

Isa crossed the threshold.

The room was cleanly divided by a glass wall lined with plants in ceramic pots in Native American designs. One half of the suite was a bedroom, the other a sitting room.

She did a double take on the bathtub—amply sized for two—nestled into a corner with windows on two sides. Marble steps led up to the kidney-shaped tub, which with its water jets could do double duty as a hot tub. She could picture a bottle of wine and platters of exotic cheese and fruit arrangements at hand on the marble windowsill.

A feeling of envy for those women he invited up here

for a romantic tryst burst through her. She wouldn't be one of them.

"Where's my room?" she asked.

He tilted his head slightly to one side and gave her an oblique glance. "You don't care for this one?"

"It's very nice, but it's obviously yours. I want a room of my own."

"Those weren't the conditions we agreed on."

She raised her chin. "You insisted on your marital rights. I agreed. You may..." She searched for words, but couldn't find any to express precisely what she had to say. The blunt truth was the only way. "You may come to me when you feel it necessary, but otherwise...." She trailed off at the enraged glitter in his eyes.

"Otherwise leave you the hell alone," he finished. "Well, sweet wife, this may come as a shock, but I can do without. And I sure as hell will before I crawl to any woman."

He ran a finger along her cheek, jaw and neck, then along the V of her blouse, his action at odds with his words.

Sensation swirled inside her, and heat gathered in her most secret places.

He leaned closer, his eyes narrowing to dangerous slits. "When *you* issue the invitation, I'll come to your bed, not a moment before."

"I won't..." she began, then faltered to a stop. She wondered what diabolical tortures she would have to tolerate during the coming year. Life had a way of getting back at those who dreamed too big.

"Yes, you will, my sweet wife." He didn't bother to disguise the thread of revenge in his voice. "Oh, yes, you definitely will."

Goose bumps rose on her scalp, her arms, her back. Even her thighs tingled at his ominous words.

"I'm not some weak-willed, spineless bimbo who will lie down and let you walk over her." She tried to sound as confident as he had.

"The challenge will be to see who can hold out longer." Giving her a look she couldn't interpret, he took her arm. "I'll show you to your room."

The other bedrooms were down a short, open hallway adjoining the kitchen and breakfast bar. He gave her the one directly across the outdoor patio from the master suite.

"I have work to do," he said abruptly, stepping back and allowing her to enter the room alone. "Can you get your stuff moved from your apartment without help?"

She nodded. After he withdrew, she paced the spacious room, which was decorated with Mexican tiles and area rugs on the shining floor. Stopping at the doors that led to the patio, she peered outside.

She could see his windows easily. She realized the corner of his bedroom visible from her windows was the one that housed the sexy bathtub built for two. A strange feeling welled up inside her when she thought of him in it with another woman. She ruthlessly held it at bay.

Looking past the covered patio, she recognized the rectangular shape of a swimming pool. A cover of some kind hid the water, assuming it had any. She laid her purse on the table in the sitting area and slipped outside.

The air temperature had rapidly climbed into the seventies in spite of the snow visible on the mountains. The desert could be unforgiving to the unwary—burning one minute, freezing the next. One had to be prepared for whatever came.

She swallowed hard and glanced at the corner window of the master suite. If she ever found her husband in that tub with another woman, she'd drown both of them! Perhaps she should make that clear from the start. Discretion started at home.

"You're what?"

Harrison smiled at the attorney, who had been a friend of the family years before he was born. In fact, he'd been named after the man. "Married," he repeated.

"My God, I think I'm going to have a heart attack." Harry Stockard clutched his chest dramatically. "Then I'm going to beat you on the head until you make sense."

"Yeah? What's the next thing after that?"

"We try to figure out how to get you out of this mess. I suppose an annulment would be too much to hope for?"

"No annulment," Harrison replied, scenes from yesterday leaping into his mind.

The hot fury returned, too. No, by damn, there definitely would not be an annulment. She was going to beg him to come to her before the year was up—

"What?" he asked blankly.

Harry sighed. "Lord, spare me another hormone-crazed client. I don't think I can take it anymore," he intoned piously with an upward glance.

"Can it," Harrison said. "You sound about as sincere as a three-dollar bill."

"Okay," the attorney said, getting down to business. He drew a notepad closer and uncapped a pen. "We'll try for a marriage agreement after the fact, although I'm sure I don't need to tell you she holds the upper hand since you've already put the ring on her finger. If we're lucky, she's still besotted with you and will sign any rights away—"

"I think we can safely forget that strategy."

Harry studied him for a long minute. Harrison met his stare, then shrugged when his advisor shook his head in despair.

"What the hell have you gotten yourself into?"

"A marriage not exactly of my choosing," Harrison admitted. "I've been caught by one of the smartest little connivers this side of the Rockies."

Harry gave his client a speculative glance. "I think we could get you off on a temporary-insanity plea. In fact, I'm damned sure of it."

"Forget it. I knew what I was doing...not exactly what I was getting into, but I knew I was doing it."

"This makes less sense by the minute. Start at the beginning and give me a point by point replay of the events leading up to the marriage." He gave Harrison a wicked grin.

Harrison started with day one and worked through the marriage and the woman now installed in a guest room at his home as his wife.

"Whew," Harry said when the story was finished, "sounds like you got yourself into a nest of vipers. She wants to bring her kid brother in, too, huh?"

"Yeah. He's in a detention center."

"My God," Harry said. "I didn't think it could get any worse. What's the kid in for?"

"Armed robbery."

Harrison was grimly pleased to see his attorney look even more pained at this disclosure. The whole story, as he told it, began to seem like a bad play. He wondered about the last act. Would it end with an annulment as Isa had promised?

Not during his lifetime.

He wasn't living like a monk for a year. She'd soon learn he meant what he said. He glanced up to see the lawyer looking at him with a worried frown. "Sorry, what did you say?"

"Do you have a list of her assets? That would be helpful in proving she married you for money in case she asks for a big settlement at the end of the year...or at the end of the marriage, whichever comes first."

"Other than her clothes and an old car, I haven't seen any assets. She lives in a furnished apartment. Oh, I do have the information on her brother." He dug the list out of his pocket. It had been on the breakfast bar when he went to the kitchen that morning. He hadn't gotten a glimpse of his wife.

Harry took the paper and read it over. "What's the most important—getting out of the marriage as quickly and painlessly as possible or checking on this young hoodlum and his problems?"

"The hoodlum."

"You've got it bad for this woman."

Harrison allowed himself a tight smile. "I find her rather...interesting."

"Oh, well, now that you put it that way..."

"Let me work out the problems of my marriage." He stood and paced to the window. In the distance, he could see the green oasis of trees that surrounded his home.

"So why did you come to me?"

"I want you to see about getting the kid released into my wife's custody...no, into *my* custody."

Harrison smiled, pleased with the idea. It gave him the leverage he needed to keep his beautiful, sharp-witted wife in the palm of his hand.

His hand tingled, reminding him of how she would feel—her hot, smooth body under his, lifting to him,

sheathing him like warm satin, her little cries of pleasure breathless and urgent.

He fought a losing battle with his libido. He wanted
to go home now, at this very moment, and claim all the
rights that marriage was supposed to confer on a man.

"I know the juvenile judge," Harry mentioned, looking at the short list of names. "We were in law school
together. I think I can get the venue changed to Reno.
That will save you a few dollars." His tone implied
Harrison would probably need all the funds he could
get to protect his future.

"Thanks." Harrison stuck his hands in his pockets
and pictured his home. He wondered what his wife was
doing at this moment. Reading? Snooping through the
house? Playing the lady of leisure?

Maggie would have her hide if Isa got in the way of
the cleaning and dusting. Now there was an interesting
combination—his conniving wife and his spirit-woman
housekeeper....

He realized Harry was giving him instructions. He'd
better listen. He might need the law on his side before
the year was up—or he turned into a blithering idiot,
whichever came first.

"One other thing," he tossed in when Harry paused.

"What?" the man who'd been his friend and advisor
for ten years snapped.

"The mining claim. Do you recall Dad ever mentioning that he'd once had a partner?"

Harry shook his head. "But old Jefferson handled
your father's affairs until he retired five years ago. I've
got a title company researching all that. They have a
guy at the courthouse today."

"Good. Hurry with that nuptial agreement. I'm anxious to see what my wife will do on that."

A horrified expression swept over the attorney. "Whatever you do, don't get her pregnant," he said.

After a startled pause, Harrison mused on the possibility. He hadn't thought about having a child, certainly not with a woman who had forced him into marriage. He wondered what Isa would say if he suggested it.

"Now that's a thought," he murmured aloud.

Two could play at this con game.

Harry cast his namesake a searching perusal, gave a dramatic groan and covered his face with hands. "Hormone-crazed, just like I thought."

"Not quite," Harrison said dryly. "Go ahead and draw up the postnuptial agreement. Let's see if she'll sign it."

Chapter Six

"I don't believe you."

Isa held up her hand with the circle of gold on her finger.

"That doesn't prove a thing," the woman scoffed.

She was tall, almost Isa's height, and about forty, maybe forty-five years old. She wore moccasin-type loafers, jeans, a checked shirt with a leather pouch on a leather thong hanging over it and a beaded headband to keep her black-and-gray hair out of her eyes. Her earrings were silver dream-catchers.

Upon letting herself in with a key and seeing Isa sitting at the breakfast bar reading the paper, the woman had asked Isa in very unfriendly tones when she planned on leaving.

Isa had decided the newcomer had to be Maggie Bird. After eliciting this information from the suspicious housekeeper, Isa had gone on to explain that she and

Harrison were married and she would be living here in the future.

Maggie flatly refused to believe her. "Harrison Stone isn't a man to get married in some hurry-scurry chapel in Tahoe."

"Well, he did."

"He didn't say anything Friday," the housekeeper said, as if this proved the lie.

"It was...a spur-of-the-moment decision."

"Harrison doesn't make decisions like that."

"He did this time." Isa picked up the rest of the Reno newspaper and rose. "I'll be in my room while you finish in here." She vacated the den and tried to tell herself she wasn't in full retreat from the scornful snort of the other woman.

An hour passed. Then another.

Isa heard the whir of the vacuum cleaner at one point. At another, she thought she heard a noise in the hall. Finally, when she couldn't stand the closed room another second, there was a knock on the door.

"Harrison's home," Maggie Bird called out.

Isa's heart nearly beat her rib cage to splinters as she stood in the middle of the room and wondered what to do.

After the scary minute, she calmed down and opened the door. She could hear voices in the kitchen—Maggie's and the pleasing, masculine baritone of her husband.

She fingered the ring on her left hand, then took a deep breath and went down the hall to face them.

Harrison leaned against the breakfast bar, which was an extension of the counter. Maggie was arranging Chinese takeout in bowls which she then heated in the microwave oven. Two places were set at the counter where she'd eaten cereal and drunk her coffee in solitary silence.

"I brought lunch," Harrison said, to explain his presence. "I figured Maggie wouldn't have enough prepared since she didn't expect an extra mouth to feed."

"Do you eat lunch here?" Isa asked.

"Most of the time."

"It saves money," Maggie put in. She set the bowls on the counter, added glasses of iced tea with sprigs of mint and lemon twists stuck on a toothpick in each one. "And it's healthier. I know all about that nutrition stuff."

"Madam," he said, indicating Isa should be seated.

Maggie ate her lunch standing at the counter, her black eyes alight with interest in Harrison's new wife. Isa felt like a strange new breed in a zoo.

"So, he married you, did he?"

Isa nearly choked on her tea. She managed to swallow and nod at the same time. Harrison thumped her on the back.

"I'm all right," she told him in annoyance.

"Just trying to help." He let his hand slide across her back, then down her arm, before he removed it.

Isa tried to ignore the trail of heat his touch had caused. It was impossible. Those hours in his arms lingered at the back of her mind like a restless spirit. They rushed forward at the slightest pretext and engulfed her with yearning that she dared not heed. Desire left her too vulnerable.

"Isa and I were married at the prettiest little chapel." He proceeded to tell his housekeeper all about it, down to the color of the roses in her bouquet and the scene from the window.

He made it sound so real, Isa could almost smell the roses again and feel the odd, excited jump of her heart when he'd slipped the ring on her finger. She touched the warm circle of metal with her thumb and pushed it around and around.

Harrison caught her hand in his and brought it to his lips. "It was a quick marriage, but there won't be a quick divorce, will there, darling?"

His eyes bored into hers, sending her a silent message. She licked her lips. "No. No, of course not."

Apparently he didn't want the housekeeper to know the truth behind their marriage. That was fine with her.

"So how come she slept in a guest room last night?" Maggie demanded, skepticism lavishly coating every word.

"Umm, yes, darling, why did you go to the guest room?" His hazel eyes gleamed with sardonic amusement.

"I couldn't sleep." She remembered something from her youth. "Your snoring kept me awake, so I went to the other room." She lifted her chin. Let him try and get out of that.

He laughed and clapped a hand on the back of her neck, sliding his long, lean fingers under her hair so he could caress the skin. "I've never had that complaint before."

She squirmed as much as she dared under Maggie's keen gaze. The housekeeper watched them like a buzzard observing a likely morsel. Isa's throat closed as Harrison toyed endlessly with her hair or stroked her neck or along her ear.

Finally, she pulled away. "You're tickling," she said by way of excuse. She ate quickly, wanting the meal to be over and the penetrating gaze of the housekeeper off her. Maggie reminded Isa of a schoolteacher she'd once had. The woman could see every thought in a person's head.

"I talked to Harry Stockard this morning. He's looking into your brother's case for us. He thinks he can get jurisdiction moved to Reno. That should make things simpler."

"Thank you. I hadn't expected anything so soon." She looked at him, then away.

Harrison had resisted the urge to kiss his wife during the meal, but when she gazed at him with the light of hope in her eyes, he lost the battle. He leaned over to her and brushed a soft kiss over her mouth, then lingered for a long minute.

"It's part of my husbandly duty," he murmured huskily. He wished he'd cancelled the day's meetings.... He pulled himself back from the abyss of foolishness over his conniving wife.

"There's gonna be someone else living here, too?" Maggie demanded, sending an annoyed frown his way.

He groaned inwardly. Maggie didn't take well to change, especially without notice. Perhaps he should have been here when she arrived and told her all the news. He could sense things were tense between the two women.

"Yeah, Isa's brother. Rick is fourteen. Isn't that right?" he asked his wife, drawing her into the conversation.

"Yes. He'll be fifteen next month."

"A teenage boy," Maggie said, as if this could be the start of the bubonic plague.

"He has no place else to go," Isa stated defensively. "I'm his only family."

"And now me," Harrison reminded her, feeling his anger soften fractionally at the fiercely protective attitude Isa displayed regarding her brother. It occurred to him that she would make a good mother.

Of his children?

His gaze went to her slender body. Harry's warning sounded in his mind. The fury rose in him. He tamped it down. If she used pregnancy to try to get something more out of him as Harry was positive she would, he'd divorce her in an instant and get custody of the baby.

Maggie broke into his murderous thoughts. "Do I fix dinner, or is she going to do it?"

"We'll continue as we always have," he told her.

"For now." Isa surprised him by putting in her two cents worth. She gave him, then Maggie, a direct, determined look that let them know she was mistress of the house. "I'll go over the menus with you each week. Perhaps there'll be other changes. We'll work them out as we go along."

He waited for Maggie to slam down the glass she was holding and quit on the spot. Instead, the housekeeper nodded her head, regally, as if bestowing a favor, but still, it was a sign of cooperation. Harrison sighed with relief that he wouldn't have to deal with a scene between the two women.

He grimaced at the irony of his life—from happy bachelor to henpecked husband in one easy move. And to further sweeten the pot, brother-in-law to a teenage hood who needed some serious straightening out.

It could be a very long year.

"Time to go back to work. I'll probably be late tonight," he told both women. After a barely perceptible hesitation, he turned Isa's face up to his and kissed her again, lighter and quicker this time. His pulse still pounded from the first kiss.

Isa climbed out of the pool and raked her fingers through her hair, pushing it out of her eyes and back over her forehead. She grabbed a towel and dried her face before going to the panel in the room that housed the pool filter equipment. She hit the button and watched the cover slide over the rectangle of clear water. This was life as she'd dreamed of living it.

So why wasn't she delirious with joy?

It certainly wasn't because Harrison bothered her. He was rarely at home. In fact, he'd worked late every night of the thirteen days since they'd returned from Lake Tahoe, including the weekends.

Not that it mattered. She was busy making arrangements for Rick's arrival and with her own work at the community center. Money was tight. They were barely covering their bills. Her job might not last long.

She had wondered more than once during the days since their marriage if the story of her short life would be told in one of those true-crime books. If looks could kill, she'd have been dead any number of times as she fled her husband's cold, mocking smile for the safety of her room.

The cool air of the house chilled her skin as she stepped inside. She jerked as she caught a movement from the corner of her eye.

Maggie gathered a bundle of sheets from the floor and straightened up. "I'm through in here. Is there anything you want from the store? I'm going after I finish Harrison's room."

"No, thanks. I have everything I need."

"Huh," the housekeeper said at that statement. She went out into the hall. "Never thought I'd see the day Harrison Stone would let his *wife* sleep in a guest bedroom. Oddest marriage I ever heard of," she mumbled to herself as she walked away.

Isa pretended not to hear most of Maggie's suspicious remarks concerning her and Harrison. The woman had thawed out a degree or two, but she viewed their living arrangements as weird and never failed to mention it at least once a day for the five days each week she was there.

After rinsing out her suit and hanging it to dry, Isa showered and dressed conservatively in a blue linen dress with a short-sleeved jacket piped in white. She wore red-and-white spectator pumps and carried a matching purse. A red-white-and-blue flag pin completed the outfit.

Harrison arrived just when she finished with her makeup. She heard his voice in the kitchen with Maggie. When she joined them, they were having a glass of iced tea, Maggie standing as usual and Harrison seated at the breakfast bar.

His dark gaze swung to her as soon as she walked in. Her heart did its usual nosedive straight to her toes whenever she saw him. She took a deep, calming breath.

He was dressed in a medium blue suit with a gray, blue and red tie. A paradigm of the business tycoon—successful, poised, conservative. All the things she wasn't. The next hour would tell if her stratagem had worked.

"You look lovely," he said, surprising her. "Ready?"

She nodded.

"It will work out," Maggie said suddenly. "I read the sacred smoke last night. It's going to be hard, but all will be well if you hold to a steady course."

The housekeeper appeared to be sincere. Isa wondered what to say to this strange pronouncement. "Thank you," she finally murmured.

Harrison finished his tea and stood. He took her arm and led her out to the car parked in the drive.

"Just what does Maggie use to produce her sacred smoke?" she asked in a light tone to break the stiff silence between them. She'd had trouble thinking of anything to say to her husband on the few occasions she'd been in his company the past two weeks.

He gave her an amused perusal. "It varies. She's the spirit woman for her tribe in these parts. I believe she takes her duties quite seriously."

"Oh." She wished she hadn't made the smart remark. "I didn't know."

"You should try talking to her sometime. She's a woman wise in the ways of life."

"Is she married?"

"No, but she's had plenty of experience. She's been married five times."

Isa used the few minutes devoted to getting in the car and buckling up to hide her astonishment. Five marriages.

"They weren't all in this lifetime," he added.

He cranked up the engine. They left the house and went to the judge's chambers where her brother's case would be discussed and a decision made. Isa's hands were ice-cold as they climbed the stone steps leading to the door.

Inside, she barely kept pace with Harrison's long stride as they went to the end of the corridor. Why, she wondered, did all institutions paint their walls green?

A couple stood in the hallway. When she and Harrison drew near, she realized it was her brother and the social worker.

"Ricky," she said. Her breath caught on a sob. Without thinking, she grabbed him and hugged him close, at that moment realizing how afraid she'd been that she'd never see him again.

"Are you all right?" she asked anxiously, drawing back to check him over better.

"Yeah, sure." He barely glanced at her before gazing down at his high-top basketball shoes.

She swallowed hard as worry balled in her throat. He seemed to have grown taller and older and harder in the three months since she'd last seen him. She spoke to the social worker, a gray-haired, grandmotherly woman.

Rick choked back the need to throw himself into Isa's arms and bawl like a kid. *Aww, man, don't. Aww, man, don't.* He kept saying it until the tears slacked off.

The weeks in detention had been the worse thing he'd ever experienced—monotonous days of classes and busywork, of fear that he couldn't show, not if he wanted to live among the bullies who tried to take the few possessions he had and the chump change he earned at the stupid chores.

Now, seeing his sister, he was about to break down in front of all these people. There'd been times when he'd thought he'd never see her again. *Aww, man...*

He pulled himself together. A man had to hang tough. "Who's he?" He gestured toward the tall guy who stood beside Isa. He was dressed in a suit, so he was probably a lawyer. Or the new husband Isa had told him about.

An old fear surfaced. Maybe he was like that other guy she'd nearly married. Maybe they wouldn't want him.

"This is my...my husband."

"Harrison Stone," the man said and held his hand out.

Rick had no choice but to shake hands. The man looked him over as if he were a slug that had crawled out from under a handy rock. He wouldn't want a kid brother around, that was for sure.

When he glanced at his sister, she smiled at him the way she used to a long time ago. It had once made the world right. The magic didn't work anymore. He still felt miserable.

The door opened behind them. "The judge is ready," a young woman informed them.

His heart plummeted, and fear washed over him. What if the judge wouldn't set him free?

Aww, man...

Isa didn't miss the suspicious appraisal Rick gave Harrison. She hoped he wasn't going to be difficult. Teenagers could be so uncooperative at times. She entered the judicial chambers.

Her husband held the door for them, then closed it and stood beside her, his arm brushing hers as they congregated in the office lined with row upon row of law books.

The judge, wearing a frown of concentration, lifted a red-edged folder from his desk. He checked it, then looked up. "I think I'm ready. Let's go into the conference room, shall we?"

They all trooped after him into the adjoining room. Isa felt as if she were going to a hanging. Hers.

The judge sat at the end of the table and motioned them to take chairs. The social worker, Mrs. Addleson, sat next to the judge. She motioned Rick to sit beside her. He chose a seat two chairs down, isolating himself from the others.

Isa and Harrison sat on the other side of the table.

"Now, run through the background for me," the judge said, after introducing himself and getting their relationships and names straight in his mind.

Mrs. Addleson opened her file and listed the facts of Rick's life. Mother died when he was five, father when he was nine. Lived with his sister, an unmarried woman, until taken into custody three months ago. Joined a gang nine months ago. Caught as a lookout in a warehouse burglary. One of the young men had a gun, making it armed robbery.

The facts sounded dismal, even to Isa, who knew the living, breathing details behind them. Fear smuggled doubts into her heart. For the first time, she faced the fact that she might lose her brother, her only relative in the world. She had a feeling that she'd never see him again if that happened.

The judge studied Rick, his face very stern. "What do you have to say for yourself?" he asked.

Rick shrugged.

The fear grabbed at Isa. "He didn't know they were going to rob the warehouse. Moe told him they were going to mark their territory. They were going to spray graffiti—"

"Let's let him speak for himself," the judge suggested. "Did you agree to be the lookout for the robbery?"

Rick slumped farther down in his seat. He mumbled something that sounded like "not exactly."

"Speak up," the judge snapped. "And sit up."

With deliberate slowness, the teenager straightened in the chair. "I thought we wuz gonna do a little spray paintin'. You know, put our marks on the territory. I didn't know nuthin' 'bout no robbery."

Isa stared at her brother in despair. His every action, including the street talk, was designed to be insolent and shout his defiance of authority. She clenched her hands together.

So close...so close to reaching the goal of having them together as a family...so close, but her brother seemed determined to throw this chance away.

The juvenile centers were nothing more than holding tanks where young toughs learned how to be real criminals. If Rick didn't cooperate with the judge, he would surely be sent back.

The familiar symptoms of panic washed over her, a queasy fear of failure that had loomed continuously before her for most of her life. She couldn't fail. Not now.

She'd promised her mother she'd keep their family intact and make sure Rick didn't quit school. They had a chance now. The goal was near. She had to say something, do something....

A large, warm hand settled over her icy cold ones.

She jerked her gaze from her brother to her husband. He was observing the scene between Rick and the judge. He released her and settled back into his chair as if watching a play.

"But once the gang was at the warehouse, you knew it wasn't just pranks, but a burglary, didn't you?"

The teenager shrugged again. "Yeah, I guess I did."

"Why didn't you leave?"

"No wheels."

"Rick," Isa said, unable to keep quiet. She fought her fears, knowing she had to be calm for his sake.

Her brother finally looked at her. She sent him a pleading glance and fought the overwhelming despair that threatened to reduce her to tears of frustration. She resolutely held on to her composure. A woman's tears meant nothing to men.

Harrison studied the little family drama being played out in the judge's chambers: the teenager, defiant and insolent as only the young can be; the judge, who'd already seen enough punks to last him a lifetime and wasn't impressed with one more; the sister.... Her role was more complex, he thought.

The mother-figure, fighting for home and family?

That image didn't jibe with the lovely blackmailer he

knew her to be. She'd been after the main chance...and he'd been it.

This was another of her acts. Her brother was probably part of her plan to bilk him out of more money—or whatever the hell it was she wanted from him and this farce of a marriage.

"Your honor, if I may speak?" she requested politely.

The judge flicked his gaze to her. He nodded.

"Things have been difficult the past few years since my father died. I...let work interfere with our home life. I wasn't there to guide Ricky in his dealings with others. All that has changed now."

"How?"

"Here, in Reno, with a different environment, things will be better. Our lives will be more...settled."

Harrison was pretty sure the judge didn't agree with her assessment. Rick didn't seem in the least reformed by his stay at the detention center, nor inclined to cooperate with his sister. The boy had slumped into the chair once more, his lips curled into the perpetual half sneer shared, no doubt, by his streetwise cronies.

Not for the first time, he wondered what he had let himself in for by agreeing to this impromptu marriage. He'd saved the mine, but what had he lost?

"Why do you think that?" the judge asked Isa.

"I'm married now. My husband and I will provide a home for Ricky...for Rick."

Harrison smiled tightly as four pairs of eyes turned his way. He nodded to indicate his agreement with his wife.

"We'll be there. Ricky...Rick...will have the support and supervision he needs."

The judge studied the three of them. He talked to the social worker about the boy's grades—excellent—his previous record—none—then pinned Harrison with a direct question. "Are you willing to assume responsibility for the boy? It's a big job and not one to be taken lightly. If I put him in your custody, you'll have to know where he is twenty-four hours a day, see that he stays in school, doesn't fall in with bad companions and keeps his grades up. Can you handle that?"

Harrison met the kid's eyes. They were like the sister's, disclosing nothing of his inner self. He turned to his wife.

The mask—that beautifully blank expression she showed the world—had disappeared. Gone was the cool, conniving woman who'd demanded marriage in return for her cooperation. He read desperation and quiet pleading in her expression.

As quickly as it had lifted, the mask slipped back into place. She turned and looked toward the window, her spine straight, her face composed. He had to admire her control.

"Yes, I think so. I'm willing to give it a try." He paused. "I agree with my wife. A stable home in a caring environment must be a better situation than institutional care." He smiled rather grimly. "We can always throw him to the sharks if he proves too much for the minnows."

His wife stirred at his deliberately cynical remark, but she held her tongue. She looked at the judge with just the right amount of anxious hope in every line of her tempting body and played her part to perfection.

Harrison let his gaze drift over her while his libido played tricks with his mind. He remembered how she'd trembled under his hands and that she'd nearly wept for reasons he didn't know.

He'd fallen for the whole act.

He cursed silently while the judge and social worker

conversed again in quiet tones. Isa's hands were locked together in her lap, the only sign of her tension. She did seem to care about her brother. He had to give her that.

A sharp pang went through him, similar to the one he'd felt when she'd laughed and chatted so gaily with his financial expert at the cabin. He mocked the envy and his wishful thinking. His sweet wife didn't give a damn about him. To her, he was the meal ticket that got her and her brother onto easy street.

Only it wasn't going to be quite as easy as they thought. Little brother would learn to do things the right way, which was to say, *his* way, or else.

"All right," the judge said, drawing their attention to him. "The court's decision is to place Ricardo Chavez under the joint care and cognizance of Harrison and Isadora Stone. For a period of one year, he will be under court observation. At the end of that time, all charges will be dismissed, provided no further charges have been incurred or are pending at that time. Do all of you understand these conditions?" He looked at each person.

Isa murmured assent immediately.

Rick, his one-sided sneer in place, dipped his head once.

Harrison nodded slowly, thoughtfully.

An auspicious beginning. This might be more than a hard year. It might be an impossible one. He already felt inclined to knock the chip off the teenager's shoulder.

"Good. That's settled, then." The judge stood and left the conference room. The four of them left the municipal building.

The social worker touched Rick's arm and told him how happy she was and how grateful he should be that he had people who cared about him. After letting him get his suitcase from the trunk of her car, she slid into the driver's seat, still talking as she closed the door. "I'll drop by in a week or so."

Harrison gestured to his wife and brother-in-law to precede him to the parking lot across the street. He breathed deeply of the sage-scented air. "Just being in there was enough to set me on the straight and narrow," he commented. "I couldn't stand to be closed up in some prison."

"It would be horrible," Isa agreed.

He checked the time. "Maggie said she'd have lunch ready by twelve. It's five past. Shall we go home?"

Isa yawned when she was seated in the comfortable luxury sedan. Its smooth leather seats invited her to curl up and take a catnap. She yawned again. She was so tired.

"How was your trip from Oregon?" she heard Harrison ask Rick.

"Okay."

"Did you come alone?

"Yeah. They had a guy put me on the plane. The social worker met me at this end," Rick explained, sneer still in place.

Isa wondered what she'd done to make him into the young tough he'd become. As a child, he'd been so sweet, with his dark, curly hair and girlish fringe of eyelashes surrounding eyes so dark they appeared black instead of brown. She and her mother had adored him. She still did.

She yawned wearily. She'd hardly slept last night, she'd been so worried. But now, thank God, she had a home for her brother. Everything would be okay....

"Isa?" Harrison shook her shoulder.

She was dead to the world. He frowned, puzzled when she didn't wake up, her mind instantly alert.

"Isa, wake up. We're home."

She opened her eyes as if drugged. He unsnapped the seat belt and helped her out. She held his arm as they went inside.

"This way," he said to his new brother-in-law, who offered no comment as he followed with his suitcase.

Maggie was in the kitchen, the luncheon ready as promised. Rick looked mildly interested at the scent of hot, spicy food.

Isa murmured something about going to her room to change. She walked off without looking back.

Harrison met Maggie's gaze and shrugged. "This is Rick. Rick, Maggie. Don't cross her. This way to your room."

He led Rick to the other guest bedroom and had him leave his luggage there.

They returned to the kitchen. Harrison pulled out a chair and sat down at the bar, which was set for three. "I'm starved. Everything looks great, Maggie."

"Thanks." She glanced in the direction Isa had gone, shrugged and passed the Mexican casserole to him, then to the kid. They ate in total silence.

Harrison wondered what had happened to his wife.

Chapter Seven

Maggie beckoned Harrison to her when he returned from the office that afternoon. He'd taken off early to see about his new family. He was afraid the kid might have done something to make the housekeeper quit by now. Apprehension stirred in him when Maggie leaned close enough to whisper in his ear.

"Your wife didn't eat lunch," she confided. "She's been in her room all afternoon."

"Where's the kid?"

"In the den watching television, where else?"

"He been any problem?"

"No. Don't worry. Troublemakers are a dime a dozen in the tribe. I can handle your brother-in-law."

Harrison winced at the reminder of his kinship with the boy. "I'll see about her."

He went to the closed door and, feeling foolish at having to knock on the door of his own wife's bedroom, did so anyway.

No answer.

He tried again, louder this time as his temper began to boil. Still no answer.

He tried the door. The knob turned under his hand. He slipped inside and closed the door behind him. He took in the room at a glance. There were few signs of her habitation—a book on the night table by the bed, the blue dress and jacket laid neatly over a chair, shoes and stockings on the floor below.

And his wife, clad in her slip and curled up in a ball in the middle of the bed, sound asleep.

He walked over to the bed as soundlessly as he could and stared down at her, wondering if this was some trick. It didn't appear to be.

She didn't move a muscle, not even an eyelid, when he sat down on the bed beside her. Her body shifted slightly, her hip meeting his as the bed dipped. The hot shock of desire jolted through him.

For two cents, or less, he'd tear off his clothes and join her....

He fought his instincts and won a brief respite from overwhelming need. He'd told his sweet wife he could live without sensual gratification, but he might regret those words before a month was past, much less a whole year.

His bitter snort of laughter didn't produce a change in Isa's consciousness. She still slept as guilelessly as a child.

However, she was a beautiful woman.

Her breasts pushed against the confines of her bra, the luscious bulges barely covered by the lacy top of the slip. Lace brushed her thighs, too, where the slip had rucked up over her knees. She had incredibly long, gorgeous legs.

He'd noticed them that day in the hot tub. He also

knew she'd used the pool. He'd noticed wet tracks on the patio one day when he came home early, but he'd never seen her in it.

His body stirred as images of them naked in the water, the sun warm on their shoulders as they came together and slowly locked into each other's arms, danced in his mind.

Gritting his teeth, he shook her gently. "Isa? Time to wake up, dream girl."

She didn't stir.

He bent over her and peered into her face. He felt her breath against his cheek, but that was the only thing moving about her. Well, he'd let her sleep. Obviously she hadn't slept the previous night...probably worried all night about her slug of a brother.

Instead of leaving, he lingered, experiencing the heat of her body all along his thigh and chest as he leaned over her. Without taking time to think, he reached out and ran his fingers along the lacy edge of the slip at her breasts.

He rubbed over the lace and down the silky material. Her nipple beaded at his touch. His breath hung in his throat.

Unable to draw away, he circled the pebbled tip and remembered sucking it into his mouth...she'd given a little cry of ecstasy when he did...and he'd moaned with the effort to hold back and not let himself sink into her womanly softness...then she'd stroked all along his sides, his back, then over his buttocks until she'd reached his hips. She'd pulled him to her, for a few glorious minutes. He'd wanted to delve into the hot satin of her body like a miner looking for gold, but she'd pulled back, her eyes cloudy with tears, as elusive as ever.

He let his hand slide down until he touched the warm

flesh of her thigh. She had a firm, athletic body, the kind he'd always liked in a woman....

Realizing what he was doing, he leapt to his feet, his breath coming in quick, hot pants. Damnation, he was worse than a peeping tom, slavering over a sleeping woman!

He strode out of the room as if the hounds of the worst hell he could ever imagine were at his heels.

Maybe they were, he reflected cynically three hours later. He banged a pencil eraser against his desk, caught it on the rebound and dropped it again while he stared out the window at the clouds hovering over the mountains in the distance.

It was late, and he was still hiding in his office.

Coward. He grimaced at the term. Afraid to go home to a woman and a fourteen-year-old? Yep, he admitted it.

He dropped the pencil, stretched and yawned, then locked up. The rest of the employees had left almost two hours ago. It was time he checked on his little nest.

The situation didn't fit his idea of how one got a wife and kid. He'd thought marital bliss started out with a man and woman. The kids came later. He'd gone from bachelor to father of a troubled teen in a single bound. Lucky him.

Arriving at home, he checked the living areas. Not a soul in sight. The scent of Maggie's stew wafted from the oven, which was turned to two hundred degrees to keep the meal warm. No signs that anyone had eaten anything, though.

Had his wife and her kid brother gone out?

He changed to shorts and a T-shirt in his room, then, barefoot, wandered to Isa's door. He noticed the kid's door was open and peered inside. The boy wasn't there, but the suitcase was open and empty at the foot of the bed, so Harrison presumed he'd be back.

Returning to Isa's door, he knocked, then tried the knob. With a sense of "been there, done that", he opened the door and stepped inside. The hair stood up on the back of his neck.

His wife was exactly as he'd left her several hours ago, still curled into a ball on the bed, still in her petticoat. She had her arms wrapped across her upper body. She looked cold.

He went to the closet and found a lightweight thermal blanket, shook it out and tossed it across her. In a minute, she shifted position, visibly relaxing as the warmth surrounded her.

She drew a deep breath which caught on a sound like a sob when she let it out. He wondered what troubling dreams she had when her lips trembled slightly.

He remembered how her mouth had often trembled under his when he'd kissed her. He'd thought it was a sign of leashed passion, now he didn't know.

It could have been an act, part of her plan to trap him into this farce of a marriage. Or maybe it was real.

His ego would like to think that, but he didn't kid himself. She'd planned her campaign to the last detail. Duty-bound to protect the family business and its employees, he'd been caught like an intrigued moth in her honeyed web.

His sweet witch of a wife was sharp. He had to give her that. She'd gotten him, the marriage and her brother out of the deal. Now it was his turn to get what he wanted.

"Move over, wife," he murmured.

Lying down beside her, he looped an arm over her waist and pulled her close. He slipped one thigh over hers and nestled his leg between hers. She sighed and snuggled close.

He nuzzled her neck, the sweet-smelling place behind her ear and down between her breasts. Not a peep out of her.

Drawing back, he studied her face.

She seemed to be deeply asleep. In repose, she looked much as she did awake. Only the lively intelligence of her gaze was missing. No emotion revealed itself in either case.

"What makes you tick, sweet witch?"

Her eyes flickered behind her eyelids briefly. Other than that, she made no move. A niggle of worry formed in the back of his mind. He pressed kisses along her jaw and onto her mouth.

No response.

Frowning, he studied her again. He ran his hand over her body, tweaked her breasts, raked his nails gently along the inner skin of her thighs. She didn't give one indication that she knew he was on the face of the earth.

He stood and walked out of the room, as frustrated as a cat whose mouse wouldn't play. He went to his room, picked up the telephone and dialed a friend from college days.

"Bill, Harrison here. I want to ask you a question, a medical question."

"Are you sick?" Bill asked.

"Not me, but...uh...my wife—"

There was startled curse from the doctor. "What wife?" he demanded in an incredulous tone.

"It's a long story."

A chuckle came over the line. "Well, I have three hours before I go to bed, unless an emergency comes up. This isn't an emergency, is it?"

"No. I don't think so. I'm not sure."

"You'd better start at the beginning," his friend suggested.

Harrison explained as quickly as he could. His attorney and godfather, now his doctor and friend knew the story of his marriage. With Ken, his financial wizard, that trio made up the three most significant people in his life, all of whom now knew his marriage was a joke.

"Hmm," Bill said thoughtfully when he finished explaining about his wife sleeping her head off while he worried that she was dying or something. "Did she take any sleeping pills?"

"Hell, I don't know."

"If she did and she wasn't used to them or hadn't used them in a while, they could put her into a comalike sleep. Did you take her pulse?"

Harrison was relieved to have something to do. "Hold on, I'll check it." He rushed to Isa's room.

She lay peacefully under the blanket and didn't move an eyelash while he counted her heartbeats.

"Sixty beats a minute," he reported into the phone by her bed. "Her color is okay. Her breathing seems normal. No rash that I can see. No fever, no chills."

"You know what I think this is?" Bill asked after thinking about it for a long minute.

"No. That's why I called you," Harrison replied, not hiding the sharp bite of sarcasm in his words.

"Battle fatigue."

Harrison shook his head, not sure he'd heard right. "What?"

"Yeah," Bill said, warming to his theory. "Battle fatigue. My father used to tell me about his Vietnam days. Soldiers who'd been out on missions for days or weeks would stumble to their cots and sleep for twelve hours, sometimes for a full day or more. One man who'd been rescued after spending six months in a bamboo cage with two other guys, slept for three days without moving. He needed sleep more than food. It's the mind's reaction to too much stress."

Isa, the cool, the beautiful, stressed out? Harrison doubted it. His silence must have said so.

"You want me to come over and look at her?"

He thanked his friend, but declined the offer. He'd keep an eye on her. Besides, he wanted to be the one with her when she awoke. In the meantime he'd better check on the brother and find out where he'd gone.

His family had left messages on the refrigerator door, the most frequented place in the house. Sure enough, that's where he found Rick's note. *Gone out,* it reported in a scrawled missive. Very informative.

An hour later, Harrison heard the entry gate open. "In here," he called. "Where'd you get off to?" he asked in friendly tones when the teenager sauntered in and slumped into a chair with the grace of the boneless young.

"Nowhere," the boy answered.

"How'd you get there?"

"Thumbed."

"Did you have supper?"

A shake of the head, eyes on the television, was the answer.

Since they had a year of living under the same roof ahead of them, he'd try to be friendly about it. "Maggie left a stew. Let's have some while we watch the rest of the game. Isa's sleeping. Looks like she's out for the night."

Rick wondered about his sister but didn't ask. He followed his brother-in-law into the kitchen and readied himself for the lecture about keeping his nose clean and not causing any trouble—*or else*. Grown-ups repeated the same advice over and over. They didn't know anything.

He loaded up the plate Harrison gave him. They returned to the ball game in the den. It felt odd, just him and a guy, eating and commenting on the plays, no lecture, no scowl of disapproval.

It made him uneasy, this palling around with an older person—Isa didn't count; she'd always been there—yet he liked it. When Harrison listened to his comments on the game, it gave him a funny feeling...like his opinion was worth something.

When the game was over, Harrison went to check on Isa. Rick hung around, not sure what to do.

He had a suspicion his sister had married because of him. He suddenly wanted it to last. This was the best home they'd ever had. He went to his room feeling scared but hopeful.

Isa woke fully alert. She knew at once whose body cupped hers, whose strong, hairy leg nestled so intimately against the back of her thigh, whose arm rested across her middle. She scooted to the far side of the bed.

Harrison stirred and opened his eyes. He returned her stare without smiling or speaking.

"What are you doing here?" she demanded, panic rising in her like bubbles in boiling water.

"I thought I had a standing invitation." He gave her a sexy once-over, then raised his eyebrows slightly as if questioning her memory.

She recalled telling him, rather arrogantly, that he could come to her if he must. She also remembered his reply. "You said you wouldn't...you didn't need...that you..." She knew very well what he'd demanded from her, but she'd thought he'd changed his mind and meant to ignore her.

"I said you'd ask." His voice dropped to a deep, husky register that stroked her senses like velvet. "You will."

The panic subsided as indignation rose. "That'll be the day." She held herself very still.

"Mmm-hmm."

He stroked along her torso with a gliding motion. Ripples of sensation ran through her. He moved closer, turning her, then he was looming over her, his thigh pressed between both of hers, his big, hard body half covering her.

His warmth spread through her, inciting longing. She gazed up at him, face composed while a riot took place in her blood.

"You are a wonder," he murmured, in a tone that was half admiring. Then he proceeded to ravish her.

He kissed her unmoving lips for long, tender moments before chuckling and moving on. He nibbled on her earlobe while he stroked around the rim of the other ear with his fingertip. Letting his fingers coast downward, he skimmed along the surface of her throat, lighting fires wherever he touched.

Isa's eyelids drifted closed. It was so tempting to relax and let him have his way...to let herself be seduced. She knew the passion he could incite in her, how beautiful it would be to share those hot caresses with him until they both exploded....

No.

She forced her eyes open. She had to keep her wits about her. "It's time to get up."

"It is?" He touched the lace of her slip and stroked along the sensitive skin there.

"I'm in my slip," she said, confused by this fact.

"You slept all yesterday afternoon. All night, too." he added, leaning down to let his lips replace his finger.

Her breasts beaded into hard points. She couldn't hide the reaction. The tiny sun flared deep inside her, and golden lava ran through her veins as he continued to touch her.

"All night?" She glanced toward the window. The slant of the sun told her it was indeed morning. "Rick—"

"In his room."

She tried to think. "I slept all through his first night here? That's terrible. I've got to—"

He kissed her into silence. "You don't have to do anything but relax. It's early yet, only six."

Against her thigh, she felt the insistent throb of his body. Her own traitorous pulse raced wildly. She understood, on some deep, instinctive level, the bond that sexual satisfaction created. If they made love, it would be harder to leave when the time came. No entanglements, that was the rule.

His hand on her leg made her start.

"Easy," he soothed in a deep, masculine purr.

She held very still as he caressed her knee and her thigh, almost to the apex of her legs. He moved back to her knee. She nearly groaned, whether in frustration or relief, she didn't know. It was unnerving.

He glided upward again, pushing her slip out of his way as he went. When it was bunched above her briefs, he swung over her, settling lightly between her legs, claiming his place as husband and all the rights that entailed.

She trembled, unable to hide her reaction.

A lazy smile flicked across his lips.

"It's only my body," she stated, needing something—*anything*—as a defense against the way he made her feel. She had to be tough and ruthless. She couldn't afford softness.

His expression cooled, although his eyes didn't. "That's all I want."

She squeezed her eyes tight, determined not to respond to his blatant sexual play. When she drew a deep breath, it fluttered in her throat, giving her away.

A tug on the strap of her slip and bra had her holding her breath. Cool air flowed over the newly exposed flesh as he slowly peeled the material from her until her breast was exposed.

"Beautiful," he said, so husky and deep, it stirred an answering need in her, despite her resolve.

She clutched the sheet in desperation as his lips did their magic, gliding lower and lower until he gathered the tip of her breast into the hot interior of his mouth and sucked gently.

A moan tore out of her throat. She put her hands against him, wanting, needing to push him away, but the will wasn't there. Instead, she allowed her hands to rest against his chest, then she pushed her fingers through the wiry hairs, aware only of the tactile feel of his male body through every contact of her skin on his. She discovered that he wore briefs and that only two layers of cotton separated them from total contact.

"What are you doing?" she heard herself ask. She really wanted to know *why*.

"Making love to my wife." He spoke against her breast, the stir of his breath cool over her damp nipple. When he raised his head, his eyes were filled with hunger. He didn't try to hide or deny his need for her. "Any objections?"

She wondered if he was trying to provoke an argument. She wouldn't give him the satisfaction. Neither would she renege on her word. "No."

A flicker of surprise darted through his eyes. He gave a grunt of satisfaction, then began moving in gentle strokes against her. She went slowly out of her mind.

When he kissed the corner of her mouth, she turned to him, unable to forego the pleasure she knew awaited her in his hands.

The kiss was wildly erotic from the start, a meeting of lips and tongue and teeth, an exploration of all the possible nuances of passion shared in this way. It wasn't quite completion but it was wonderful. And it fired the desire for total melding.

When she thought she could stand it no longer, he broke the kiss. "Do you want more?"

She blinked up at him. Disappointment hit her. He was trying to get the upper hand, to control her, but she wouldn't play those games. Life was too serious. "I won't beg," she told him. "Never."

His smile was slow. Light gleamed in his eyes, taunting her with the desire she couldn't deny. "Do you want more?"

"Do you?" she challenged, barely able to keep her wits.

He studied her for a long minute. It was insulting. "I want a hell of a lot more, dear wife, but I don't think I'm going to get it, at least not today."

With this strange explanation, he pushed himself upright on one elbow as if to move away. His gaze swept over her. He lingered to run a fingertip over her breast again, watching as the nipple contracted predictably.

Anger, with herself for not being able to resist him, with him for making her respond, surged within her.

"I'm not a child to be swayed by physical appetites," she told him even as she shivered in anticipation.

"No," he agreed, "you're not a child." He paused and listened for a second. "I think your brother is up.

We'd better have a family meeting and decide what to do about him." He rose in one smooth movement and climbed out of bed, leaving her chilled without his body heat surrounding her.

She pulled the blanket to her chin. "He has to be enrolled in school. I checked. There's still six weeks to go before it's out for the summer."

"He'll be a sophomore this fall?"

"Yes."

"Good. I have an idea." He stepped into a pair of shorts, fastened them, then slipped into a T-shirt. "Let's have breakfast, then we'll talk."

"About Rick?"

Harrison paused at the door. "And other things," he promised, a decisive set to his mouth.

She wondered what he had in mind while she showered and dressed. She hurried to the kitchen after smoothing on a light coating of moisturizer and makeup.

Rick was eating a bowl of cereal at the breakfast bar. Harrison leaned against the counter in Maggie's usual place, a mug of coffee in his hand. Isa greeted them both.

"Good morning. You look lovely," Harrison commented.

Rick didn't say anything.

"Doesn't your sister look lovely, Rick?"

Rick glanced up. "Yeah, sure," he mumbled. The only sound in the kitchen was the ticking of the wall clock and the munch of cereal as the teenager continued eating.

Isa tensed for a scene as Harrison's eyes narrowed while he watched her brother finish the meal and shove the bowl aside.

"Around here, we put our dishes in the dishwasher when we finish," he remarked. His gaze flicked to her. "Coffee?"

"Yes, please."

Rick got up, shuffled around the counter in a pair of flip-flops and stuck his bowl and spoon inside the dishwasher. He picked up a glass from the sink and put it away, too, then he went to his room.

The edgy moment passed. Isa relaxed while she had toast and a glass of orange juice.

Harrison glanced at the clock. "I have a conference call at nine. Do you need help in getting Rick registered for classes?"

"No. I can handle it. Mrs. Addleson, the social worker," she added at his blank look, "will be coming over this week to see how things are going."

The tension bubbled while he considered this. "Will it be a surprise visit?"

"I don't know. She said she'd see us this week."

"I'll probably be working late several nights. You can call me if she shows up."

Isa nodded. He'd hardly been at the house at all during the two weeks of their marriage. She'd often felt she'd lived most of her life alone, yet she hadn't realized how empty a house could be until she'd rattled around in this one, alone for hours on end. It was odd to miss a husband who didn't want her.

"I'll stop by your office at noon," he added. "My attorney has some papers for us to sign."

"All right."

He watched her while she sipped her coffee, then blotted her lips on a napkin before he put his mug in the dishwasher and left the room. A minute later, she heard the growl of his car's engine when he backed out of the garage.

PLAY SILHOUETTE'S
LUCKY HEARTS
GAME

AND YOU GET

- **FREE BOOKS!**
- **A FREE GIFT!**
- **AND MUCH MORE!**

TURN THE PAGE AND DEAL YOURSELF IN...

Play "Lucky Hearts" and you get.

YOURS FREE!

This lovely necklace will add glamour to your most elegant outfit! Its cobra-link chain is a generous 18" long, and its lustrous simulated cultured pearl is mounted in an attractive pendant! Best of all, it's ABSOLUTELY FREE, just for accepting our NO-RISK offer.

...then continue your lucky streak with a sweetheart of a deal!

1. Play Lucky Hearts as instructed on the opposite page.
2. Send back this card and you'll receive brand-new Silhouette Special Edition® novels. These books have a cover price of $3.99 each, but they are yours to keep absolutely free.
3. There's no catch. You're under no obligation to buy anything. We charge nothing—ZERO—for your first shipment. And you don't have to make any minimum number of purchases—not even one!
4. The fact is thousands of readers enjoy receiving books by mail from the Silhouette Reader Service™. They like the convenience of home delivery...they like getting the best new novels BEFORE they're available in stores...and they love our discount prices!
5. We hope that after receiving your free books you'll want to remain a subscriber. But the choice is yours—to continue or cancel, any time at all! So why not take us up on our invitation, with no risk of any kind? You'll be glad you did!

The Silhouette Reader Service™—Here's how it works:

Accepting free books places you under no obligation to buy anything. You may keep the books and gift and return the shipping statement marked "cancel." If you do not cancel, about a month later we'll send you 6 additional novels and bill you just $3.34 each plus 25¢ delivery per book and applicable sales tax, if any.* That's the complete price—and compared to cover prices of $3.99 each—quite a bargain! You may cancel any time, but if you choose to continue, every month we'll send you 6 more books, which you may either purchase at the discount price...or return to us and cancel your subscription.
*Terms and prices subject to change without notice. Sales tax applicable in N.Y.

She checked the clock. "Time to go," she yelled down the hallway. No answer. "Rick, it's time to go."

He sauntered out of his room. "I'm not going. I've decided to quit school."

"What?"

"Yeah, I'll get a job—"

"You're too young to quit school," she reminded him. "You have to go. It's part of your parole."

"I'm not on parole." He gave her a fierce frown.

"You heard what the judge said. For the next year, you're in a sort of trial period. You have to go to school."

His thin face took on a mutinous cast, but he didn't argue.

"Are you going to wear that?" she asked.

He had on ragged jeans and a black T-shirt. "Yeah."

"Then let's go."

He was silent on the ride to the school. Isa didn't force him into conversation. She remembered what it had felt like—changing schools every couple of years to follow her father's schemes. Life had been hard.

"You'll need lunch money," she said when they parked at the high school. She dug into her purse and gave him twenty dollars. "That should cover supplies, too. I've already arranged for your books. The office will have them."

"Yeah, sure." He swung out of the car. "I can go in by myself. You don't have to baby-sit me."

She hesitated, not sure if she could trust him, then felt guilty for the thought. If she didn't show her confidence in his honesty, then who would?

"Okay," she said, forcing a smile. "The center is three blocks down this street. I'll give you a lift home."

"I'll be okay," he muttered. He slammed the door and sauntered off before she could question him further.

Worried, she backed out of the parking space and headed for her office. Really, she had nothing to worry about. She'd signed all the school papers a week ago to enroll Rick in classes. The counselor understood his circumstances and knew to call the community center if anything happened.

Not that anything would. This would be a turning point in their lives. When he settled in, Rick would do well here. He'd be happy and well-adjusted and all those things she wanted so desperately for him. Life would be good from now on. She'd see to it.

On this optimistic note, she entered the office well before ten and worked on the bills and usual problems that cropped up during the day. The program director, the only paid person on staff besides her, stopped by at noon.

"We need better equipment," Sidney told her.

"There's no money."

He frowned in disgust. "Throw a fund-raiser. Hey, I hear you're married to one of our benefactors. Ask him."

She resented his cavalier attitude. "Harrison already pays half the mortgage on the building. If you think you can get more out of him, you ask. I won't."

Sidney shrugged. His gaze became speculative. "You two had a rather rushed wedding, didn't you?" His eyes skimmed down her body, making her uncomfortable.

"No. It was exactly what we planned," a male voice answered before she could.

Jerking around, she spied Harrison leaning negligently against the door frame, his suit jacket draped over his shoulder, his tie loose and his collar open. He held a white paper bag.

"Lunch," he announced. His frigid glance at the director dismissed the man.

Sidney, perched on the corner of the old desk, got to his feet. With a nod to her, he walked out.

Harrison moved into the room to let the other man pass. "The center in financial trouble?"

"Always." She sighed wearily. "That's been my main job—find ways to keep it going."

"Why wouldn't you agree to ask me?" He set the bag on her desk, hooked a straight chair with his toe and yanked it closer so he could sit beside her.

"You already do enough." She clamped her lips together. Defending him wasn't part of the job description. "Besides, I didn't think you had any extra money to invest in a surefire losing proposition."

"I don't," he said frankly. "You should have told him you plan to keep the money in the family. For you and your brother."

Her mouth gaped at this flat statement. "That's not true. I only want what's due us. Nothing more."

"A home for a year, then an annulment, right?"

"Yes."

"And half the mine earnings, assuming it has any by then?" He filled a paper plate with Chinese food and started eating. He raised his eyebrows when she didn't follow suit.

"I want what rightfully belongs to my family, nothing else. I am not a fortune hunter."

"Sorry. A misjudgment on my part, I'm sure. It happens when a man is blackmailed into marriage."

His smile was so icy, she shivered. Well, she could hardly expect him to think well of her. Only time would prove she was an honorable person. Sort of.

"My attorney prepared some papers." He took them out of his jacket pocket and handed them to her. "I've already signed."

She opened them and started reading. "These are a…a prenuptial agreement."

"Postnuptial, actually."

"What is the agreement?"

"That at the end of a year, you leave without further claims on me or my assets."

She sighed with relief. He was going to give her the year. That was all she needed. She grabbed a pen and flipped to the back page.

"You might want to read over the asset lists. I wasn't sure exactly what yours were."

His eyes raked down her, pausing at strategic points, while he continued to eat calmly.

Keeping her face perfectly blank, she read over the contract and signed it without arguing. In essence, she'd agreed to leave with what she'd brought into the marriage.

She handed the document to him. His eyes searched hers as if suspecting a trick.

"No argument?" he asked. "No addendum or challenges?"

"No, I think you got it about right." Her assets were her clothing and her six-year-old car. She couldn't help but grin. "Five thousand dollars might even be stretching my net worth by a thousand or two."

The narrow-eyed suspicion in his gaze as he continued to study her was joined by wariness and other emotions she couldn't identify. He probably detested the very sight of her, but that was okay. She could handle it.

She knew how she felt—relieved. She hadn't liked him thinking of her as a gold digger. It had weighed on her conscience more than she'd realized before this moment. Her signing the contract proved she was merely a blackmailer.

The thought was so absurd, she laughed without thinking, startling her husband who was taking a bite of an egg roll at that moment.

Chapter Eight

Harry looked at the signature on the agreement. "This probably isn't worth the paper it's written on."

"Why not?" Harrison demanded, irritated by his godfather's gloomy mien.

"Because it was signed soon after the marriage when things were all sweetness and light between you two. She could break it in a minute. In Bono versus Bono—"

"Speak English," Harrison interrupted.

"When Cher sued Sonny, she won." Harry sat back in his chair and waited for Harrison's next question.

Harrison eyed the portly attorney warily. "Just tell me what happened," he requested in a resigned tone.

"Sonny had Cher sign an agreement when they were married that essentially said he controlled everything she did for life. After the divorce, when she agreed to do a show, he pulled the prior agreement on her, saying she couldn't do anything without his permission. She took him to court."

"And won," Harrison finished.

"Right. No one can control another person's life forever. There has to be an escape clause."

"I thought that's what this was." Harrison pointed to the agreement lying on the desk.

Harry picked it up and studied the two signatures at the bottom of the third page. "Watch out," he warned. "She signed this too easily, with not one change."

"Yeah. She probably knows every divorce case in history and has a plan to make sure this agreement doesn't stick in court."

"A woman of foresight," Harry said with a wistful sigh. "When am I going to see her again? That one time you rushed her past my table with hardly more than an introduction was much too brief. I don't remember what she looked like."

"A dark-haired Madonna." Harrison smiled briefly. "With a heart full of dollar signs."

"Except where her kid brother is concerned. She has a soft spot there, I think."

Harrison snorted in disbelief. "Or it could have been a ruse to make her appear noble and all that. I intend to discover the real person behind the facade."

Harry scowled. "You looked pretty ruthless when you said that. Don't do anything...ah...untoward."

"I wouldn't dream of it," Harrison vowed, placing a hand over his heart. A sense of recklessness joined the cold fury. His lovely wife was a challenge he couldn't ignore. He'd know her inside out before the year was up.

Isa swept the living room with a critical eye. The house looked nice. She moved the vase of fresh flowers to one end of the narrow table behind the sofa and repositioned the group of figurines.

"That's the third time you've done that," Harrison remarked. He sat on the sofa, watching the evening news on PBS.

The social worker had called thirty minutes ago and said she'd stop by on her way home that evening. It was after seven, and on a Friday night. The woman kept long hours.

Almost as long as her husband. He'd taken it well when she'd called his office and said he had to come home at once. She'd wanted him to be there to present a solid domestic front so the social worker could see how happy they all were. He'd arrived ten minutes after she'd called.

She could have kissed him when he came in the door...and might have if he hadn't been his usual cool, sardonic self toward her. That had saved her from making a fool of herself, thank goodness. It wouldn't do to go soft toward him.

Harrison had changed to chinos and a deep blue polo shirt before joining her in the living room. The blue in the shirt brought out the blue in his eyes, which contrasted handsomely with his dark hair. His male aura seemed especially alluring tonight. It stirred memories of passionate moments in his arms when his touch had almost shattered her reserve....

She pulled her gaze from her husband and surveyed the room again. Maggie kept the house in perfect order. She couldn't fault the spirit-woman there. If she'd only keep her mutterings about the marriage to herself, Isa would have been perfectly pleased with the housekeeper.

Fat chance of that ever happening. Maggie expounded on all subjects that crossed her path, especially strange marriages.

"What are you smiling about?" Harrison asked suddenly.

Isa bent to fluff a cushion that didn't need it. "Maggie. She told me today Rick couldn't be all bad. He doesn't play rap music at full volume like her nephew does."

He chuckled, and they exchanged an amused glance. It cracked right through her defenses. Longing flooded her heart. She couldn't look away.

He watched her, too.

She sensed the wariness in him. He wasn't a man to expose his heart in the best of times. In their nearly three weeks of marriage, he'd shown her only the outer workings of his mind.

He treated her with a distant courtesy, except when passion or anger surfaced. Then he could be cruel, tormenting her with needs she couldn't deny. She didn't know if the cruelty was intentional or not.

Unlike other men she'd known, he was too hard to read. He would make a formidable poker opponent.

The doorbell chimed.

"I'll get it." Harrison went to the door and returned with the social worker.

Isa's mouth went dry. "Mrs. Addleson," she managed to say. "It's nice to see you."

"Please, call me Martha."

"I'm Isa. You remember my husband, Harrison?"

"Of course. I'm delighted to see both of you again." Her lively gaze swept over the living room and what she could see of the kitchen.

"Would you like something to drink? I have coffee made. There's spiced tea, too."

"No, thank you." She got right down to business. "Where's our young man?"

Isa felt the flutters of panic grab her stomach. "In his room. I'll call him—"

"Don't bother. If you'll show me the way, I'd like to talk to him for a few minutes."

"Of course. His room is down the hall here." Isa led the way. "Rick, Mrs. Addleson is here to see you." She stepped back so the woman could enter Rick's room.

Isa saw that it was still neat. Her brother sat at the desk. A textbook was open, and he had a paper in front of him that he was writing. Good, he was doing homework.

"I...my husband and I will be in the living room...if you need us," she added lamely.

Mrs. Addleson nodded, a dismissal.

Isa retreated down the hall. She heard the murmur of voices as the social worker greeted Rick and went into the room. The door closed behind her.

In the living room, she sank into a chair and stared at the TV screen without seeing it. She locked her hands together and waited for the outcome of the interview.

"Relax," Harrison told her.

She smoothed the black knit of her slacks. "I hope—"

"What?" He flicked the TV off.

"I hope my brother remembers his manners," she confessed.

"Umm, yes, teenagers do seem lacking in that department for the most part. Sometimes it's hard to believe they grow up to be credit-card-carrying adults, isn't it?" His tone was wry, but not worried.

She pleated the material, then smoothed it, over and over again. Minutes crept by. A glass of the spicy iced tea that Maggie had made for them appeared in front of her.

Harrison gave her the glass, then returned to his seat. She was aware of his gaze while he drank from his glass. He chose a cookie from the plate he'd placed on the coffee table.

"We might as well be comfortable. This may take a while," he commented and snapped half a cookie off in one bite.

She controlled her resentment. After all, it wasn't his future that was on the line. Looking at her watch, she wondered what Mrs. Addleson and Rick could be discussing. Her brother didn't say more than five words to her in a day.

At last, footsteps sounded in the hall. The social worker returned. "I'll take that tea now, if you don't mind."

Isa jumped to her feet.

"Sit still, darling. I'll get it." Harrison ambled into the kitchen while Mrs. Addleson took a seat on the sofa and opened her notebook on her lap.

"The weather seems to be warming up fast after that storm earlier this month, doesn't it?" she asked.

"Yes, it does." Isa tensed when the woman glanced around, then wrote several notes on a page.

Harrison returned with the tea.

"Thank you." Mrs. Addleson took a drink and sighed in heartfelt delight. "That's delicious."

"Have a cookie," Harrison invited. "Maggie Bird makes the best peanut-butter cookies this side of the mountains."

Mrs. Addleson beamed. "I know Maggie quite well. She's helped me more than once with youngsters from her tribe." She selected a cookie. "I probably shouldn't eat this. I haven't had dinner yet."

"I'm kinda hungry myself," Harrison confessed.

Isa realized he probably hadn't eaten, either. She

hadn't thought about it before. Guilt rushed over her. Before she could apologize, Harrison spoke again.

"Maggie roasted a turkey breast yesterday. How about me and you rustling up a sandwich, Martha?"

He stood and waited. Martha hesitated, then rose, closing the notebook as she did. "That sounds like an offer I can't refuse." She went to the kitchen with Harrison.

Isa sat in the living room in irritated surprise. She'd had answers prepared for any questions the social worker might ask. Now they were scattered like bowling pins.

"You want anything, hon?" he called from the kitchen.

She joined the other two. Martha sat at the breakfast bar. Harrison rooted around in the refrigerator. He set the turkey platter on the counter, found the fat-free mayo, pickles, pickled peppers and lettuce and added them to the fare. A loaf of bread and a bag of chips followed the other items.

"See if Rick wants something," he suggested.

Isa, after giving Harrison a wary glance, went to invite her brother to the impromptu feast.

This was not how she'd imagined the evening would go. She'd envisioned them chatting politely in the living room for a few minutes. She'd serve coffee, tea and cookies. Rick would have milk with his cookies.

Martha would see that they were an ideal American family. She'd give them high marks, write up a glowing report in her notebook and leave, satisfied that Rick was in good hands.

"We're having turkey sandwiches. You want to join us?" Isa asked, pausing at the open door of his room.

"I guess. Sure." He shrugged as if he couldn't think

of anything better to do and unfolded himself from the desk chair.

She realized her baby brother was as tall as she was.

"Please, remember to be polite," she whispered, frowning in worry. His attitude might not sit well with Mrs. Addleson.

He glowered at her, but made no comment as they went to the kitchen. She wondered again if she was handling him wrong.

Laughter greeted her when she and Rick entered the comfortable room. With a start, Isa realized that while Martha had gray hair, she really wasn't so old...late forties, maybe.

She stole a quick study of the other woman. Actually, the social worker could be in her early forties.

A funny feeling settled in her chest when Harrison continued with some story he was relating. When he finished, his deep chuckle joined with Martha's laughter. The blend of masculine and feminine merriment was oddly intimate.

The whole scene was, Isa realized with a jolt. Harrison was making the sandwiches, and Martha was slicing them in half and putting them on plates, along with the condiments and chips. There was nothing about her that suggested the grandmotherly type, which had been Isa's first impression at the courthouse.

The funny feeling coalesced in her throat. She swallowed hard, then smiled coolly when she saw Harrison watching her.

He brought another chair to the breakfast bar that wrapped around the end of the counter. "I think everything is ready."

Isa took her usual seat, and Rick sat to the left of her. Harrison politely waited until Martha took the chair where she'd sat before, which was on Isa's right, before sitting in the extra chair. He was directly across from Isa. Martha was between them. Again, that funny feeling attacked Isa.

"How did you get into this line of work?" Harrison asked their guest.

"My mother. She was a social worker, too, before she retired last year. I was worried about her after my dad died a couple of years ago. Now she's on an exotic honeymoon cruise with her new husband and is studying the martial arts." Her happy laugh made those around her want to laugh, too.

Harrison chuckled, clearly enjoying the woman. "She seems to have found a new lease on life."

"Yes. If I weren't such a nice person, I'd be green with envy." She wrinkled her nose when she grinned.

The confession was spoken with such wry good humor that the admitted envy took on the shine of an endearing human trait instead of a fault.

While the other two chatted like long-lost friends, she and Rick ate their sandwiches in silence. Harrison was the most charming of hosts, drawing their guest out expertly, laughing at her humorous stories as she related her early experiences.

Even Rick laughed a couple of times. Isa forced herself to join in, too. She didn't want to appear a curmudgeon.

An hour passed.

"My goodness, look at the time. I need to get home," Martha finally said.

"One more thing. Is there any rule against Rick driving as soon as he's old enough?" Harrison asked.

Rick's head snapped up in astonishment. Isa stared at her husband, not sure what to expect. He glanced at her, then Rick before turning back to the social worker.

"Not as long as he has a valid driver's license," she said.

"He'll be fifteen soon. That's old enough for a day permit. Is it okay with you for him to drive?"

"If he accepts the responsibility that goes along with driving." Martha's tone was stern.

"He will." Harrison raised one eyebrow as he glanced in Rick's direction. "Right?"

Rick hesitated as if unsure what to say. "Uh, yeah. Sure." His expression was wary, yet so hopeful, Isa found it painful.

"Isa's car needs work. We'll rebuild the engine this summer, maybe get a paint job to brighten it up." Harrison reached into his pocket and took out a set of keys. He handed them to Isa. "You can have the red car. Rick can drive yours when we get it in prime shape."

"The one in the garage?" she asked stupidly. The sleek two-seater sports car that looked like a cool million?

"Yes." He smiled at Martha. "Let me see you to your car." He ushered the woman out, leaving Rick and Isa standing there.

"You gonna let me have the car?" Rick asked. He looked as if he expected her to say no, as if she'd take away the promise that Harrison had made.

She realized that during much of his young life that was exactly what had happened. Their father had made promise after promise to them. *This* time things would be different. *This* time they were going to strike it rich...get a horse...a new bike...a house so they could have a real home....

She clenched the keys until they hurt her palm. She couldn't deny her brother the promised gift of a car, but she wasn't going to take anything that wasn't hers.

"Maybe. On your birthday," she said. She nearly added "if you behave," but held the words inside.

"Like, wow!" he said. He surprised her with a bear hug, then picked up the dishes and put them in the dishwasher without being asked. He looked carefree and happy for the first time in ages.

Isa blinked fiercely as a rush of love for the brother she'd raised hit her. She wanted to go to her room and mull over the evening, but she had a few things to say to her husband first.

Isa heaved an exasperated sigh. She'd waited forever for Harrison to return to the house. After he'd stood out in the chilly desert night air and talked to Martha for a good forty-five minutes, she went to her room to change clothes. Upon returning to the kitchen, she found the lights out and the house locked up. He'd come in and gone to his room.

She glared out the window across the patio toward the master suite. The lights were on in there.

Tightening the belt of her robe, she took her courage in hand and went to confront him. After crossing the dimly lighted atrium, she stood outside his door, afraid to knock.

Perhaps she'd better confront him in daylight…and in the kitchen rather than his bedroom at night. But before she could scoot back to her room, the door opened.

Harrison stood before her, a towel draped over his shoulder. That was all he wore.

"Oh," she gasped. She couldn't keep her gaze from roving over his tall, powerful body. He was overwhelmingly masculine. "Oh," she said again, unable to think of another word.

"I'm going for a swim," he announced. "Care to join me?"

She resented his cool tone, the overlay of cynical humor directed at her. Heat swept up her, down her, all the way through her. For a horrible second, she thought she might faint.

Then she remembered he'd been talking to another woman before going to his room and deciding on this late swim.

"In the future," she said, keeping her eyes on a potted fern next to the door, "I'd appreciate it if you'd discuss anything that involves my brother with me before mentioning it to him. Or anyone else."

There. That was all she had to say. She turned to leave.

A hand caught her arm and whirled her around. Her shoulders were seized, and she was lifted almost off her feet.

"You sanctimonious little prude."

"I beg your pardon," she said in the haughtiest voice she could muster. She pulled the ragged edges of her righteous dignity around her. After all, *she* hadn't stood out in the moonlight for an hour talking to some stranger.

Their noses were no more than two inches apart. She stubbornly held his glare, giving as good as she got.

He smiled suddenly. It only made him look more dangerous—a wild, fierce savage that she was beginning to think she had misjudged when she'd made her grand plans.

"You should." He let her down slowly. His hands rubbed up and down her arms gently, belying the harshness of his tone.

"Well, I don't see why. I have nothing to apologize for." Really, he was impossible to understand.

"For your evil thoughts." He snorted in exasperation. "It's a strange turn of events when a married man has to go for midnight swims in order to rest. I have a wife who's supposed to take care of my marital needs."

Her anger surged at his accusing tone. "I really don't care to discuss this."

He laughed, a soft, sultry sound that scared her more than his fit of temper. "You're right. Words solve nothing between us. Maybe it's time you lived up to your part of our bargain."

She gazed up at him in stony silence. She became aware of the silence surrounding them, of the late hour, of moonlight falling like silver on the patio, of the fact that she was in her nightgown and robe and he was in...nothing.

"Wasn't I the perfect host tonight? Didn't I make every effort to ensure Martha saw a sweet little family nest here? She was impressed as all get-out by our happy home. Don't I deserve a reward for that?"

"I...I..." Her throat closed. She shook her head.

"No?"

His breath fanned over her face. She detected the scent of liquor. "You've been drinking," she accused.

"I had a brandy, thinking that might help me sleep. It didn't. After reading a bit, a swim seemed like a good idea. Not expecting company at this late hour, I didn't consider a suit necessary." His laughter was harsh. "Imagine my surprise at finding my wife, dressed for bed, outside my door. I naturally assumed she had come to honor her marriage vows."

She made a strangled protest, which he ignored.

"A man might be forgiven for leaping to conclusions, or having a libidinous thought or two, or reacting with visions of the sensual delights awaiting him in the marital bed in such circumstances," he concluded.

"I didn't come here to join you in bed."

Stiff with her own indignation, she couldn't help but note that his fury didn't interfere in the least with the reaction of a certain body part belonging to him. Even as he expounded on his grievances, his pure masculinity called to her, inviting her to join him in those sensual delights he'd mentioned.

For one traitorous second, her memory supplied images and sensory perceptions from their tryst at the mountain cabin—how smooth and strong he'd felt to her, how gentle his every touch had been, how she'd loved the contact of flesh touching flesh and the hot sliding friction of his body against hers. She'd loved his every caress....

"This is ridiculous," she finally managed to sputter. "I can't stand here all night arguing with you." She tried to ease out of his grasp.

He grinned wolfishly. She thought inanely of Little Red Riding Hood. *What big teeth you have, Grandma.* His hands didn't tighten their hold, but neither did he let her go.

"Oh, no, sweet wife, not yet."

Before she could figure out what to do, he gripped one arm and herded her outside. He reached into the equipment room and hit the button for the pool. The cover slid out of sight.

When Isa tried to hold back, he simply pulled her forward with his greater strength.

"I don't want a swim," she whispered furiously. She glanced toward her dark bedroom windows and the safety she'd left when she ventured out on her self-righteous errand. She'd been insane to confront him at this late hour.

"It'll be good for you." His smile was ruthless while he waited for her acquiescence.

She set her jaw stubbornly. Whatever game he was playing, she wasn't going to join in. She was the injured party here, and he was going to listen to what she had to say. The next instant, she was swept up against his chest.

A mixture of panic and intense excitement bubbled in her, a cauldron of emotions that were beyond her control. She trembled from head to foot when he stopped by the pool.

"With or without your clothes?" he asked with fake courtesy.

Time stilled. She could hear crickets chirruping, her heart beating, the deep slow breath he took.

"I'll scream."

"And wake your brother?"

She bit her lip, uncertain of her husband's intent. His eyes gleamed in the moonlight, his expression resolute.

They had reached a turning point. Each knew it. She should protest, but she couldn't utter one word. She couldn't think—

He set her on her feet, then reached for the ties to her robe. She stayed still as he removed the garment. His touch was light, but she felt it throughout her body as if boulders were rolling over her, crushing her...her resistance...her good sense.

His hands went to her hips. His fingers gathered the material of her nightgown. He paused when the gown's hem was clasped in his hands, her legs bare to the night chill.

"Are you going to fight me?" he asked.

He didn't sound angry anymore. He was no longer taunting or cynical or amused. She heard the husky cadence of desire, felt it in the tension of his hands against her flesh, sensed it in the heat his body radiated.

When she didn't answer, he slowly moved his hands

upward, taking the gown with them as he did. She let him. The material slipped over her head. He dropped it on top of the robe.

Panic rose. Before she could flee, he lifted her up and took two running steps, then plunged into the water. She kicked away from him. His skin grazed hers as they surfaced halfway across the moonstruck water.

He tagged her on the shoulder and swam toward the deep end. His laughter drifted over his shoulder, mocking, challenging.

The panic turned to fury. So he wanted to play games with her. Turning, she thrashed after him, determined to catch him. All thoughts of protest and common sense flew out of her head.

They played in the heated water for ages, leaping and diving and tagging each other, sometimes touching, a glide of flesh on flesh as they passed. They raced from end to end of the pool.

Finally, they sat in the shallow end, breathing fast and deep. He took her hand and coaxed her into the shadows cast by the roof overhang of his bedroom. He kissed and caressed her for a long time. Then, as if in a dream, he positioned himself between her thighs and entered her.

He cushioned her head by placing his arm under it on the step. She rubbed her hands over his back and hips.

"This isn't real," she said, reaching for a defense to shield her trembling heart.

"I know." He kissed her to silence.

Chapter Nine

Harrison lay in bed and contemplated the brightening of the sky as dawn broke over the desert. He felt lethargic this morning, with the sated morning-after laziness that comes from a night of intense sensual gratification.

Stretching, he winced at the stiffness of muscles well-used during the night's unexpected activities. The memory of those erotic moments swept over him, bringing a wave of heat that pooled in his groin.

The stir of desire emphasized the emptiness of his bed. His sweet deceiver of a wife had declined to stay with him. Perhaps it was against the rules for black-mailers to spend the whole night with their victims, he mused, mocking the need that taunted him. However, making love before sharing a leisurely breakfast would be a nice way to start the weekend.

No early-morning romps for this married couple, he

concluded stoically, the heat of anger intermingling with the fires of passion. He threw the sheet off and climbed out of bed. After a quick shower, he dressed in shorts and a T-shirt and headed for the kitchen. Isa was there.

She wore slacks and a white blouse and looked as prim as a schoolmarm. But he knew better.

He knew how buttery-smooth and hot she became when he touched her, how she writhed beneath him and held him close and gave him kiss for kiss, how she gave little cries of welcome when he entered her. Twice during the night, he'd turned to her. Twice, she'd accepted him....

"Good morning," he said, unable to keep the huskiness from his voice. "You working today?"

She turned to him, her face composed into the pleasant mask that revealed nothing. No trace of last night's passion lingered in her mist-shrouded eyes. The night might never have been.

Fury mingled with desire. He contemplated sweeping her into his arms and carrying her back to bed like some hero in a melodrama. Except he'd probably get frostbite if he tried anything so foolish.

"Yes," she replied. "I need to go over the receipts and work on the financial reports."

"So dedicated," he murmured, fighting the need to challenge her frigid pretense that nothing had changed between them.

She poured him a cup of coffee. "I found a waffle iron and made waffles this morning. Would you like some?"

He considered the question. She acted as if she might be trespassing by using the kitchen utensils.

"Yes." He watched, his mood darkening, while she

moved about the kitchen with the fluid grace of a dancer.

As usual, she avoided looking directly at him after that first quick meeting of the eyes.

"Thanks," he said when she put the plate in front of him and moved a pitcher of warm syrup close. "This is nice," he added.

Isa had resumed her seat and was looking at the morning paper, as cool and remote as a moon goddess.

This isn't real, she'd said during their wild lovemaking.

No, it wasn't, but he recognized the possibilities.

He now understood why some morning meals had been full of jocularity and teasing between his own parents during his youth. He now knew why the subtle touches and meetings of their eyes had made him feel funny inside—happy and secure, yet with an overlay of excitement that he'd been too young to comprehend at the time. Now he did.

That's what marriage should be, what he'd wanted and expected to find, until he'd been trapped by the coolest little conniver this side of the Rockies.

The anger beat through him. A need to break through her icy facade swept him to the brink of control. "I've been thinking."

"I hope it wasn't too much of a strain," was her quick comeback. She had a sharp mind, he had to give her that.

"Nah, hardly any at all. I was thinking, with a full year of marriage, that should be plenty of time."

She laid the paper aside and picked up her coffee cup. "Time for what?" She took a sip.

"For a child." He waited for his words to sink in.

She blinked at him...once...twice. A rosy shade of hot pink climbed her neck and face. "You don't have to worry. There won't be a child. I'll stick to my end of the bargain. At the end of a year, you'll be free, with no ties of any kind."

He kept his voice soft. "You don't understand. I want a child, an heir. A man should get something from his marriage."

"You...that's impossible—"

"Why? We're husband and wife. I thought that was the usual way to get a family...as opposed to getting one ready-made like buying a suit off the rack." He waited for her reaction.

Raw emotions flashed through her eyes too fast for him to define. When she blinked, they were gone, replaced by the fathomless mist that hid her inner thoughts so effectively. So much for shock tactics. He wasn't any closer to understanding her than the day she'd pulled her blackmail trick on him.

"A child wasn't part of the deal. I already told you I won't try to trap you that way."

"An honorable blackmailer, huh?" He paused, cynically amused by the irony of the situation for a moment.

She stiffened, but refused to rise to his baiting. "If you wish to put it that way, then yes. I will keep my word."

"Good," he murmured. "Good." He picked up the paper.

Isa mulled over the conversation. She couldn't believe he'd want a child with her. This was a ploy, a psychological probe into her mind to find a weakness. She'd already given him one insight into her. She came apart when they made love.

She couldn't help it. During those exquisitely mad moments in his arms, she couldn't hide behind a false smile. In those moments, she was exposed and vulnerable. It frightened her.

A woman had to stay in control. She had to be strong to take on a man of Harrison Stone's caliber and win. She couldn't afford the luxury of being soft...or in love.

Seeing him watching her with a speculative gleam in his eyes, she rose from the chair. "You don't want a child," she accused. "You want control. You want to see how far you can push. There's nothing you can do to make me give up. You'll be free in a year and not before." She walked out.

In the garage, she started her car and backed it out. Before hitting the remote control to close the garage door, she stared at the red sports car. It, too, was part of some game he was playing with her, a temptation dangled before her, like last night when he'd taken her into the pool.

And she'd gone with him without a murmur of protest.

A woman couldn't be weak like that, melting in his arms, letting moonlight brew impossible dreams. It was beyond foolishness to let herself believe in fairy tales. She sighed dispiritedly.

One year. Surely she could make it.

Isa paced to the office window and back. No sign of Rick. This was the third time he'd been late that week. When she'd questioned his tardiness, he'd mumbled that he'd been hanging out with some guys. She hadn't met his new friends.

During the month he'd lived in Reno, he hadn't brought anyone to the house. It had been the same when they lived in Oregon. He'd kept his life and friends separate from hers.

His birthday was coming up. Maybe they could have a party with some of his classmates in attendance.

At six, she heard the outside door open. Rick sauntered into the office a minute later.

"Oh, good, you're here. I was getting worried." She gave him a sharp glance, but he said nothing. "I have a meeting with the center's board of directors tonight. It shouldn't take more than a couple of hours. I'll give you money to take a cab home. Maggie is off today. Can you manage dinner on your own?"

"Sure." He pushed a lock of hair out of his eyes.

She resisted the urge to tell him to get a haircut. There were so many directives she wanted to spout. *Straighten up. Look at me when I talk to you. Stop mumbling.*

Once he'd been the dearest little boy, climbing into her lap with a favorite book he wanted her to read, nestling his head of fine, dark curls against her while he waited for the story to begin, so trusting it had made her heart ache.

Their mother had been weak after his birth, and Isa had taken care of the new baby from the start. One of the last times he'd allowed her to hold him had been when she'd explained their mother's death while their father was out drowning his sorrow at a local tavern. He'd been five years old.

She swallowed the pain of those memories. The past was done. "Your birthday is coming up. I thought we might do something special. How about a pool party with a cookout?"

"That's for kids."

"I know adults who like them, too," she responded mildly. She removed some money from her purse. "You could invite your new friends and some classmates you'd like to get to know better. Surely there's some sweet young thing you find interesting—''

"No party." He took the bills and stuffed them into his pocket, then edged toward the door, ready to be off.

She understood his eagerness to be gone. She hadn't liked hanging around her father and his cronies. When she'd been fourteen, adults had been the enemy. "I'll see you when the meeting is over," she said to his back as he left the office.

Slumping into the rickety desk chair, she worried that she was handling Rick wrong. She'd read psychology books and talked to his school counselors. She'd tried to be understanding of his needs, his doubts, his hormonal upheavals.

Sometimes she wanted to slap him upside the head and have done with it. But she could never bring herself to be brutal with him. She still remembered the scared child who'd looked at her with tears in his eyes and begged, "You'll stay, won't you? You won't go away to heaven like Momma did, will you?"

"Of course not. I'll never leave you," she'd promised. She could remember the feel of his arms and legs wrapping around her, clinging with all his might.

Her vision blurred.

Forcing back emotion, she picked up the folder with the financial records and looked over the dismal budget for the center. It was time for a meeting.

The five directors straggled in within the next fifteen minutes. After greeting each one and serving coffee, she handed out copies of the report she'd compiled during the past month. They perused them in silence.

"Unless we can come up with more money, this will be our last year," she said when they'd finished reading.

"Why haven't you raised the money? That was what we hired you for—"

"No," Isa corrected with a weary smile. "I was hired to manage the center."

"And you've done a good job," one of the other directors asserted. He turned to the sour-faced woman who'd spoken first. "Ms. Chavez raised enough to pay off our most pressing debts. That calling campaign worked, but we can't do it every month."

"No, we can't," agreed another. He had the well-fed appearance that goes with being a bank president.

For two hours, they argued each idea brought up. When they started debating whose fault it was that the center was in dire straits, Isa decided it was time to intervene.

"I have a suggestion," she offered.

Five pairs of eyes focused on her, each pair reflecting the hope of instant reprieve.

"Let's close for the summer. That would cut down on expenses enormously, since we wouldn't have to use the air-conditioning. In late fall, when the weather cools, we could start a new program. The amateur theater group draws the biggest crowds in the winter, so it makes sense."

"What about the loan from this year? The bank is pressing for more than just interest payments."

"There's a trust fund. If we use it—"

"But that's our building fund," the woman protested. "This place needs renovating."

"If we don't have a building, we won't need a building fund," the bank president commented dryly.

"There's enough to pay off the mortgage and the current loan," Isa told them. "Once those are paid off, we can start an improvement project and raise new funds. Our admission rates for the plays are low. We could raise them by five dollars."

"People won't show up. They're used to cheap entertainment at the casinos."

Isa nodded. "We'll have to plan a promotion campaign to make the plays attractive to visitors. I think we should try convincing some of the stars from the casino shows to do cameo appearances as a public service to help finance our youth programs. It would be fun for them and gain publicity for us."

Footsteps sounded in the hall.

Isa paused to see who was there. Since it was Wednesday, there was no play scheduled that night and rehearsals for a new production hadn't started due to a lack of funds. They couldn't afford the electric bill.

Harrison appeared at the door. "My wife is a great planner. Her plans often come to fruition, I've found." He leaned his shoulder against the door frame, his hands in his pockets, and smiled all around at the little group.

"Wife?" the one woman on the board questioned.

"Didn't she mention it?" Harrison asked with charming innocence. "I'm crushed. We've been married almost six weeks, six wonderful weeks," he added with a smoldering glance at her.

Heat rushed into her face as the directors peered at her with varying expressions of surprise.

"Congratulations," the banker said, springing to his feet to shake Harrison's hand. The other three men did the same.

"I don't believe I saw an announcement in the paper." The woman eyed them as if she thought they were lying for some nefarious reason.

Harrison snapped his fingers. "Damn, I forgot about that. Darling," he said in a sweet reprimand to Isa, "you should have reminded me."

"I didn't consider it necessary."

He came to her and looped an arm around her waist,

pulling her against his side. "All brides want their new marital status known, don't they? It sort of says, 'look, I won.'"

The hard edge in his voice caused the others to glance at them in puzzlement. Isa smiled with forced calm.

"And so I did." She held up her left hand and displayed the simple gold band as if it were the Hope diamond.

Her husband brought her hand to his lips and kissed it tenderly. All the while, his eyes issued a challenge that only she could detect.

She saw the pattern of the coming months. Harrison would taunt her about their blissful marriage in front of others, so subtly they'd never catch on. In private, he would ignore her as he had for the past month. That night in his arms might never have been. He seemed to resent their marriage more now than he had the day of the wedding.

"Let's see what we can do about your problems here." He took Isa's copy of the report and settled in her chair.

She stood there in growing exasperation.

He patted his knee and gave her a roguish grin.

"Huh," she snorted and pulled up another chair. She looked over his shoulder as he read her neat rows of figures, the lists of assets and liabilities, the net worth and balance sheets.

"Very impressive," he said when he finished. "I didn't realize I'd married a female financial wizard."

"I have a degree in business management."

"Ah, yes, college. Where you were engaged."

She couldn't decipher the dark look he turned on her. "For a brief summer. That's about as long as a man's promises last."

"But a woman's last for a year?" he inquired in his Ivy League drawl.

The five directors stopped reading the reports and watched them with avid curiosity.

Isa felt the telltale heat slide into her face. She had started the verbal sparring with her remark about men, she admitted, but he didn't have to remind her of their bargain and, even worse, the words they'd had about it weeks ago.

A child. I'd like a child.

There couldn't be one. Children involved long-range plans. Eighteen years of commitment. They only had a year.

She still hadn't figured out why he'd suggested it. To torment her with what might have been and what he'd have someday with his real wife was cruel.

"I agree with Isa," he said after a thorough study of her numbers. "You need a stable financial base to work from. I think I can spring for the same amount I've been paying on the mortgage for another year. That would provide a basis for the youth program budget if the building was paid for. J.T., you think you and the bank can match that?"

Harrison had issued a direct challenge, one the banker couldn't refuse without losing face with his peers gathered around the desk. He shrugged in defeat. "I'm sure we can."

"Good. Mrs. Barns, you're involved in your late husband's charity foundation that started the community center. Can you convince the trustees to provide the seed money for a new building fund?"

Her eyes darted around the group as if looking for someone to pass the buck to. "Well, I suppose," she finally agreed.

"Great. James, the attorney association sometimes involves itself in charities. They should be good for a donation and perhaps some legal advice. How about talking to them?''

The attorney nodded obediently.

''We can get some of the building trades to donate time and expertise in reconstructing the building, maybe bring in some of the high school kids to help out and make this a real community effort,'' Harrison finished. ''Has anyone checked about getting the building on the National Register? That would give us all kinds of credibility.''

''Oh, I hadn't thought of that,'' Isa exclaimed, seeing the possibilities broaden.

''That's why two heads are sometimes better than one.''

His eyes sent another message as they skimmed over her. Her breath caught in her throat as she thought of their two bodies entwined in the pool.

''Yes,'' she admitted, ''for some things, two are better.'' For establishing a home. For raising a family.

He nodded, then he concentrated on questions from the directors as they explored the ideas he'd tossed out.

Isa kept the minutes of the meeting while Harrison directed the discussion. During her time there, they'd tried to heap all the responsibility on her. Harrison had neatly turned the tables on them. Each director went home with a task to perform before the next business meeting.

''What?'' he asked when they left.

She continued her study of him. ''You know very well.''

He pushed his chair back so he could stretch his long legs straight out and crossed them at the ankles. With his thumbs thrust into his pockets and a smile hovering at the corners of his mouth, he exuded triumph.

"Did I do good?" he demanded.

"You know you did." She looked down at her entwined hands. "Thank you. I could never have handled them half so well."

There followed a beat of silence.

When she glanced at him, it was to see a somber expression on his face, not the self-satisfied grin she'd expected. His gaze roamed over her in a moody perusal. He paused when he met her eyes. "It was nothing."

His voice reached right down inside her and started the tiny sun to blazing. Its warmth spread through her, warming her in places she hadn't realized were cold.

"Shall we go home?" he asked. "Are you through here?"

"Yes." She checked her watch. "It's after ten. Rick will be wondering about us. I told him I'd be ready to go at eight."

"How did he get home?"

"I sent him in a taxi. Thank you for stopping by." She stored the reports in the file cabinet, locked it and her desk, then picked up her purse. "Okay, I'm ready."

She followed Harrison on the drive to the house. When they were parked in the garage, he asked, "Why aren't you using the other car?"

"I'm afraid to," she confessed lightly. "It's too expensive. If I had an accident, I couldn't pay you back for a long time...a very long time."

He snorted impatiently. "I have insurance," he reminded her. "As my wife, you're covered. In fact, you and your brother are on my health and accident insurance now."

"I didn't intend...it isn't necessary..."

"Of course it's necessary. You're my wife. Rick is part of our family. I changed to a policy that took in all of us."

She didn't know what to say. It made her feel funny, as if she and Rick really belonged, as if the three of them had formed a real family. "Thank you."

He gave an impatient snort as he unlocked the door, but he didn't say anything more. They went into the dark, silent house.

"Rick doesn't seem to be home yet," she said. All the usual worries surged into her mind. He could be hurt, dead, lying on the side of some road, run over by a speeding driver—

"Isn't tomorrow a school day? It isn't some kind of holiday, is it?" Harrison asked.

"I don't think so."

"We're going to have to establish some rules around here on hours and such." His tone was hard.

"I'll talk to him," she said quickly.

"Perhaps I'd better."

"No, please. I'll handle it." She waited while he studied her for a long minute, then he nodded.

He covered a yawn, stretched, then headed for his room. "I'm off to bed. Care to join me?" he tossed over his shoulder.

"No, thank you." She sounded primly formal, as if refusing an invitation to a party of uncertain reputation.

"Too bad." He didn't sound at all as if he meant it.

She hurried to her room. Later, dressed for bed in her long nightgown, she wondered at the heaviness that clung to her. It wasn't as if she'd invited her husband's attentions.

Was she one of those women who protested because she wanted to be swept off her feet like a pliable reed that could be bent to anyone's will? Of course not. She had other things to do—like wait up for her errant brother.

She wondered what she could say to Rick that would

make him see the danger in his actions. A feeling of hopelessness washed over her, dampening her usual optimism.

Fatigue pulled at her as she went to the study and flicked on the television news. She wondered if Harrison was doing the same in his room. There was a set in a wall unit across from his bed.

Longing rushed through her before she could close the door on those thoughts. Her husband had been the most incredible lover, warm and tender, all the things a woman could desire.

She forced herself to read a magazine so her mind wouldn't stray to things that would never be. Sometimes it was so hard to go on pretending. Sometimes she was invaded by the most incredible longing....

Sighing, she stretched out and rested her head on the padded sofa arm. Rick would surely be home soon.

Isa woke with a start and rose to a sitting position. She listened. She heard a noise as someone entered the house.

"Rick?" she called. "I'm in the study."

He appeared at the door a moment later, hands thrust into his pockets, his posture defensive. "Yeah?"

"It's after midnight," she said accusingly, unable to stem the note of anger.

He shrugged.

"Where were you?"

"Out."

"Alone?"

"With a couple of guys."

"From school?"

He shrugged again.

She persisted. "Were they classmates?"

"One of them was."

"And the other?"

"Just a guy I met."

She summoned all the patience she could muster. "Where did you and your friends hang out until midnight?"

"We were at one of the casinos."

"You're too young," she began, then realized he stood as tall as she did and could easily pass for twenty-one.

"I didn't play or anything. I just watched."

"You shouldn't have been there." she said slowly, searching for words. She laid a hand on his arm. "You had other things to do. Like be here at home when I arrived. I was worried."

Rick couldn't meet his sister's eyes. "Sorry," he mumbled. He wanted to tell her Moe, who he'd thought was his friend, was in town and threatening him, telling Rick how he'd get him in trouble, what he'd do to her and Harrison if Rick didn't go along with his orders.

Moe was planning on robbing a bunch of stores. He wanted Rick to recruit a gang to do it. Rick wanted out. He didn't want his family to get hurt or his friends to get in trouble.

Once more he wanted to throw himself into his sister's arms and have her make everything all right the way she used to. But he couldn't. It was his problem. He'd figure out what to do.

"That isn't good enough," Isa told him. "If Mrs. Addleson had dropped in, what would I have told her, that you were hanging around the casinos?"

"She didn't, did she?" A sudden vision of having to return to the detention center shook him. *Aww, man.*

"No, but that's beside the point."

He summoned the tough-guy stance that got him through hard times. His sister had enough troubles. He couldn't throw himself at her and cry for help. She'd confront Moe without a thought to her safety. He had to get out of this on his own, but first, he would have to deflect her attention to something else.

"Why are you worried? You got a good deal here, married to a man with all kinds of money. You don't have to work at all, but you don't even act like a wife."

Even as she gasped, he knew he'd gone too far and that he'd hurt the only person who'd ever cared about him. He didn't know what to do. He swallowed as words knotted in his throat. *Aw, man, aw, man.*

Isa controlled herself with an effort. "You don't know anything about it," she said in a low voice.

"Well, it's weird that you two don't share a room. What kind of marriage is that?"

"None of your business. We're not here to discuss my marriage. It's your behavior that's the problem. From now on, you will come straight home from school. Maggie will tell me if you don't," she warned when he gave one of his defensive shrugs. "You'll be in your room at nine every night. Lights out by ten."

"I'm not a kid—"

"Then stop acting like one. If you get in trouble, you could be sent to a juvenile center. Is that what you want?"

"I'm not going to get into trouble. I can take care of myself." He wouldn't look at her.

She wanted to yell at him. She wanted to tell him she'd lost the chance to find any kind of happiness with her husband by forcing him into marriage and saddling him with a family that was nothing but trouble. But when she looked at her brother, she saw a young person halfway between child and adult, unsure of his place in the scheme of things.

Sorrow rooted out her anger. His pretended indifference was a shield against an indifferent world, a world he'd learned not to trust. Their father's word had been as solid as a straw in the wind.

When she reached out to touch his shoulder in sympathy, he shied away as if she had struck at him. The sorrow deepened.

"We have a good life here," she told him, unable to keep the tremor from her voice. "You're smart. You can get a scholarship to college, be anything you want. Don't throw it away."

For a second, he looked as if he might cry, then the boy was gone, replaced by the hard-knocks kid. "Yeah, sure. Is it all right if I go to bed now?"

"Yes," she said through a constricted throat.

She watched him walk away in the loose-boned, effortless way of the natural athlete. He had so much potential. There were so many ways it could go wrong.

After returning to her room, she tried reading to put her mind at rest so she could sleep, but it was impossible. She flicked out the light and sat in the dark, her thoughts roaming from her relatively happy childhood—when her mother had been there to do the worrying about the family—to her own adolescence that had been filled with work and worry, to the present when she'd thought things would somehow be wonderful for a year.

What wishful thinking that had been.

The loneliness of the past nine years washed over her. She'd learned never to cry, but lately she'd felt constantly on edge, and sad, so very sad. She didn't understand herself at all anymore.

Rising, she laid her book on the table and went to the window. The cover was off the pool and a dark figure stood beside it, the lithe, masculine body cast in silhouette against the underwater pool lights.

Her heart pounded, echoing in her ears as if it beat in a great empty cavern. Harrison raised one hand in an invitation to join him, but there was no one outside with him.

She realized he knew she was there, hiding in the dark, watching him....

Her hands went to the tie on her robe and paused. She pulled in a ragged breath, let it out in a shaky sigh. Without any conscious decision on her part, she moved to the patio door, opened it and stepped out.

The night air rushed over her, cool and sensuous. The sun flared inside her. When she stood no more than a foot from the moonlight-clad male figure, she pulled the ties and let the robe drop from her.

He waited, his eyes drinking her in, his mouth curved in a half smile. She looked at him expectantly. He waited.

She eased one strap off her shoulder, then the other. The gown slithered down her body. Her skin was so sensitive, she could feel the slightest vibration in the air. She shook her hair back and looked at him.

He waited.

Slowly, like someone in a dream, she held her hand out.

He clasped it in his and turned toward the pool. Together they took the plunge.

As soon as they came up for air, she touched him, wrapping her arms around his chest, her legs around his hips. She felt his surprise, but she didn't care. She needed his strength.

She clung to him with all her might. "Make love to me." She didn't know whether she was begging or demanding. "Make love to me now."

"All right." He locked his arms around her and climbed out of the pool.

She lifted her head from his shoulder. "Where are we going?"

"To our room."

His eyes met hers. Consent was given and an agreement was reached in that moon-blinded moment.

In their room, he made love to her for a long time before he let the final moment roll over them in wild delight.

Chapter Ten

Isa woke to wet kisses being pressed over her face. She kept her eyes closed, afraid to face the day.

"I know you're awake," Harrison murmured, with a chuckle vibrating over the words.

She opened her eyes. A hot flush crept into her face as she remembered her wanton conduct. *You'll have to ask,* he'd told her soon after their wedding. She'd done more than that. Last night, she'd begged.

Make love to me, she'd said by the pool. *Please, please, please,* she'd said in his bed during their lovemaking.

A sheen of perspiration coated her as embarrassment sent the heated blood pounding through every part of her. With it came the desire and the need to lose herself in his arms again…and again…and again.

"I…it's time to get up."

"Um-hmm," he agreed, taking nips along her ear,

then down to her throat. He threw one leg over both of hers and pulled her close, tucking her into the curve of his body. Against her thigh, she felt the growing force of his erection, warm and hard and wholly masculine.

Against her will, she recalled the tenderness of his touch, the strength that he'd so carefully controlled as he'd brought her the gift of exquisite pleasure.

"Your skin reminds me of gardenia petals. It was my mother's favorite flower."

"I'm allergic to gardenias."

He ran a finger between her breasts in gentle swishes. "I'll remember that," he promised. He bent and kissed the very tip of one nipple.

Tingles shot through her like Fourth of July sparklers. Her skin where he'd touched her contracted into a hard bead.

"Am I dreaming?" he asked, kissing the corner of her mouth.

"A nightmare," she quipped, grappling with her slipping composure. "Probably something you ate."

At his amused look, she blushed wildly.

"I've thought of waking up with you for so many mornings, I'm afraid this is another fantasy."

"I think…"

He skimmed lightly down her body.

"We should…"

Pausing, he ran his fingers through the tight curls.

"That we should…"

Her mind went completely off track when he dipped into the intimate folds of her body. She was moist and ready for him.

"So do I," he whispered against her lips as he bent to kiss her again. "We should…very definitely…"

By the time he moved over her, she was aching with eagerness for his total caress. He brought her to a shattering climax before letting his own hunger have its way.

Afterward, he held her without speaking. She fought a terrible need to cry. Her eyes moistened against her will.

"Tears?" He looked puzzled. "Are you sad?"

She shook her head helplessly, embarrassed by the show of emotion. "No. It's just..."

"Guilt?" he suggested in a wry tone.

She felt the return of his suspicion, heard the skepticism in his voice that only moments before had been husky and tender. The wrench of her heart told her she was in danger of doing something stupid...like thinking the passionate moments between them meant something. She moved out of his embrace, needing distance in order to regain control.

"No," she denied. "I've kept my part of the bargain."

A wave of raw fury swept over his face. For a second, he looked as if he wanted to choke her. Instead, he swung out of bed. "And did it quite well," he said coolly. "Shall I have Maggie move your things over?"

His eyes darkened when she hesitated. "I'll do it," she said quickly. He nodded, then headed for the shower.

"The flowers look nice. Do you think we planned for enough food? There will probably be thirty people. Unless everyone from the center brings a guest, then we might have more."

Isa surveyed the table laden with Maggie's special hors d'oeuvres, which were Mexican in flavor—fajita roll-ups, *poco polla fundidas,* flavored chips and six different dips varying in spiciness from mild to singe-your-eyebrows hot. Maybe she should have planned a couple more varieties.

"There's plenty." Maggie removed cocktail quiches from the oven. "I have extra of everything in the freezer. If we run low, I'll pop another package in the oven."

"Oh, good. That's good." She rearranged the platters of food and aligned the napkins once more.

"Relax," Maggie advised. "You're as nervous as a cat at an old folks' home."

Isa looked at her blankly.

"You know—old folks, rocking chairs." Maggie rolled her eyes when Isa continued to stare at her. "Rocking chairs, cat's tails, as in getting caught under?"

"Oh," Isa said. She paced between the kitchen and the living room, checking for anything they might have overlooked. "Yes, I am a little nervous. This is my first party."

"What do you mean, first party?"

She smiled at Maggie's doubting tone. "You know— guests, food, laughter. It's the very first I've given."

"Ever?"

"Yes. Do you think we should switch the table centerpiece with the one on the—"

"It's fine. You had birthday parties when you were a kid, didn't you?"

Isa shook her head. "Never had 'em, never went to one, although I was invited to a couple. I couldn't afford a gift. Oh, speaking of money, where did I put that deposit receipt?"

She'd gone to the center earlier, collected the meager receipts from various activities and put them in the night deposit at the bank before hurrying home to help Maggie with the party. Harrison hadn't arrived yet.

Today had been the closing day of the community center. She and Harrison were having a farewell get-together for the staff of volunteers who had made the center possible.

She found the receipt in her purse and put it in the folder on the desk in Harrison's room…their room. She paused by the bed. She and Harrison had shared it as husband and wife for ten nights, counting this one.

In spite of Maggie's approval that they now had a "real" marriage, her future seemed more uncertain to her. She had a few details to close out next week, then she'd be out of a job. She didn't know what she'd do after that.

Maggie handed her a platter when she returned to the kitchen and loaded more quiches onto a plate covered with a red napkin. "Relax," she advised again.

"Does…has Harrison had parties here before?" Isa asked, coming back for the next dish.

"He has a Christmas party for the office every year."

"Here?"

"Uh-huh. Oh, and a pool party on the Fourth of July."

"For the office people?"

"It varies, who he invites."

"Oh. Is this what he usually serves? Do you think he'll like the color scheme? Or the flowers? Oh," she repeated, flying to the door, "they're here."

Maggie's laughter followed her.

Her husband, handsome in a dark suit, led the way and their guests followed him, the sounds of their voices mingling with the birdcalls in the night. Isa tried not to appear nervous.

"We're here," he said and surprised her with a kiss.

Harrison noticed the glaze of—panic?—in Isa's eyes as she clutched his arm, then let go and turned to their guests. He watched his lovely wife in puzzlement until he saw her slip into her usual mode—the cool, unflappable woman who had everything under control.

Except when she came apart in his arms.

Desire stirred in him. So what else was new? He'd wanted her from the moment they'd met.

His wife was incredibly beautiful in a flame-red dress that was sleeveless and dropped to a low point between her breasts. She wore a simple gold chain around her neck and matching ones in her ears. She wore no rings other than her wedding band.

Soft music played on the stereo. A couple started dancing. Others joined in. Ah, a good idea.

Before he could wind his way through the crowd, the director of the youth programs grabbed Isa and pulled her into a fox-trot.

He stopped, frowning as prickles of emotion darted through him. Nah, he wasn't jealous. No way. He backed up to the breakfast bar and watched while the strange feeling gnawed at him. He was annoyed that someone else had claimed Isa, that was all. He'd wanted her first dance.

Maggie replenished the refreshment table, then returned to the kitchen. She stood in her usual place on the other side of the counter and observed the crowd.

"Did you know this is your wife's first party?" she asked in a low voice. "Her first ever."

He flicked the housekeeper a glance of inquiry.

"She was so nervous that everything wasn't just right. She wanted it to be perfect…for you."

Somehow Maggie, who had been his friend for years, had gone over to Isa's side during his brief marriage, especially since Isa had moved her things to his room.

"I'll be sure to tell her everything was wonderful,"

he promised, thinking of the hours ahead. A slow warmth spread through him.

He noticed the volunteer basketball coach, a young man about Isa's age, had stolen her away from the director and was now leading her into the intricate series of steps of a tango. To his surprise, she did them flawlessly.

Others stopped dancing and gave the couple room to perform. The blond-haired Adonis and the black-haired Venus danced as if they were longtime partners, moving effortlessly to the music, the beat a part of them as they performed an exotic pantomime of seduction, refusal and finally surrender. They ended the dance in a sensual embrace with Adonis holding Venus bent back over his arm, his body half covering hers.

"Watch it," Maggie cautioned. "You're in danger."

"Of what?" he asked, unable to take his eyes off the pair.

"Of falling in love with your wife." She laughed as the blood flowed into his face. "Don't ruin her party."

He got a grip on the rage that pumped through him. He didn't even understand what he was upset about. So his wife and some young, good-looking guy had danced as if they belonged to the same body, so what?

Meeting Maggie's eyes, he saw a warning in them.

"It'll work out," she told him, "but you must deal with other problems between you first. Then, I think, you will find your own true love."

"Been reading smoke signals again, Maggie?"

She smiled. "Yes. The future is yours...if you know how to take it."

He gave a snort, exasperated with her cryptic portent of things to come. "See if you can read the smoke a bit more clearly. I need directions."

"Start with the brother."

She went to the refrigerator and removed a gallon jug of punch. While she refilled the bowl, he thought about her last statement. Maybe it was time he stepped in with Rick. He'd left the boy to his sister's care, but maybe the kid needed a man's touch. He knew one way to control teenagers.

Striding across the room, he deftly plucked his wife from the arms of the Adonis and pulled her into his. He looped her arms around his shoulders and put both arms around her waist, holding her with no space between them as a slow love-ballad filled the night.

He danced her out the open doors onto the balcony and into the shadows, ignoring the teasing calls from their guests as he did. He wanted to hold her. It was as imperative as breathing.

"It's a good thing I know you'll be in my bed tonight," he whispered for her ears only.

She drew back to gaze up at him. "Why?"

"Because I'd be jealous as hell otherwise."

"Of Tony?" Her expression was one of disbelief.

"A man likes to know his wife finds him more desirable than other men."

"Oh, I do." Her eyes sparkled. She lowered her lashes and brushed against him, flaunting her awareness of the passion he couldn't hide.

"Jezebel. You'll pay for that…later."

"Promises, promises…"

When she laughed, he found himself intrigued all over again by the woman he'd married. Temptress, wife, defender of her little family. She was also a blackmailer who had dollar signs in her heart. He'd better remember *that* when he got to feeling soft toward her.

Isa handed the keys over to the night watchman who guarded the buildings on the block. Leaving the community center locked and empty seemed as terrible as abandoning a friend in need.

"See you in the fall."

"Take care, Mrs. Stone." He signed and dated a receipt, then handed it to her. After stuffing the keys in his jacket pocket, he zipped it closed.

She walked down the block to the parking lot where the red sports car which she now drove was parked. Harrison was there.

"How about dinner somewhere quiet?"

The invitation was delivered with a moody frown. The ever-present anger flickered. Only in bed, when the passion flared bright and pure between them, did his distrust of her recede.

Sometimes his attitude stung like a paper cut, but only time would convince him he could trust her. When the year was up and Rick was released, she'd go quietly. Then Harrison would know she had always intended to keep her word. That he knew she was honorable was important to her.

"That sounds lovely." She got in his car when he opened the door. "I feel like I'm playing hooky."

Harrison studied her while snapping his seat belt. "You've never had many chances to skip away from responsibilities and have fun, have you?" he asked on a different note.

She was instantly on guard. One thing she didn't take was pity from anyone. She'd had enough of that from well-meaning neighbors while she was growing up. She wondered what she'd done to elicit it from her husband.

His mouth curved into a sardonic smile. "Relax. This isn't going to hurt a bit."

"I didn't expect that it would," she said stiffly.

"Always direct and to the point," he commented, glancing her way and back at the road. He headed south of town and made a series of turns onto some obscure streets before parking in front of an Italian restaurant. "One of Reno's best-kept secrets," he said, helping her out and into the tiny place.

Inside, a man played a violin while another accompanied him on the piano. A set of drums stood unused at the side. A haunting rendition of "La Dolce Notte" tugged at her heartstrings while the hostess led them to a table.

Framed posters from Italian operas hung from every available wall space. Dark green cloths covered the tables and votive candles shone through ruby canisters covered with net. It was very romantic. Harrison ordered kir royales for them.

"Champagne with black-currant liqueur," she surmised after taking a taste from one of the fluted glasses.

"Right. To my beautiful wife," he said softly, "who blushes each time I compliment her. Now why is that? A man might think you were an innocent instead of a cunning deceiver."

The illusion of romance faded, although a part of her wanted to pretend all was wonderful between them. Another part was on guard. Her husband's eyes probed hers as if looking for all her secrets. It would be so easy to tell him, to let herself grow used to sharing life with him, to think they were in love....

No. Love played no part in her plans. A year, she reminded herself, then she and Rick would have to go. For a moment, she was frightened as she thought of the future. She remembered the loneliness of the past and the responsibility that her fiancé hadn't wanted to shoulder. He hadn't wanted a ready-made family. Neither would Harrison, not for keeps.

A splatter of applause broke the tense moment. A man, familiar to her, walked over to the piano. He and the two musicians consulted, then, having agreed upon the selection, he burst into song. His voice was powerful and moving.

"Why, he's from one of the casino shows," she exclaimed, recalling his face on a poster. "The visiting lead from a Broadway musical. I'm impressed."

"Yeah, word gets around. Lots of stars wander in here for a few hours of relaxation. They can sing, put on a skit or ignore everybody. It's up to them."

"I see."

"It's a place a man can enjoy a quiet moment with the special woman in his life."

"Or even his wife."

"Someday I'm going to slip past that sharp tongue of yours," he murmured, "and leave you speechless."

"You already did that. Remember when you accepted the...um...marriage proposal?"

"I haven't forgotten a word of our wonderful courtship," he assured her.

She gave him a suspicious once-over. She didn't trust him when he was in this overly congenial mood, which he'd been in for days now. Since she'd moved in with him.

Maybe it was sex. They made love every night. He came home from work early and kept regular hours. They ate at six-thirty, watched television or read or swam until ten, then went to bed. He'd invited Rick to join them for a swim several times.

To her surprise, her brother had done so twice. He seemed to like being with her and Harrison. At times, when they shared popcorn and watched television together, they felt like a family.

Rick had also been late getting home twice that week. Worry nibbled at the edges of her mind. He'd probably been at the library where he'd said he was. She had to show some trust in him, but she still worried.

"Relax," Harrison advised, as if he could read her thoughts. "Rick was home when I stopped by to check on him. I kept him company while he ate dinner. We're going to start rebuilding the engine of your car tomorrow."

"That's good of you." She searched for words. "I think he needed someone, a man he could trust...a...a role model...like you," she finished, becoming flustered at his intent stare.

"Praise from my wife?" he queried. "I'm overwhelmed. I thought you pictured me as a black-hearted devil out to take crusts from babies' mouths."

"I do." She'd guard her tongue from now on. It didn't pay to expose a soft side to her enemies.

"Ah, shall we order?" he asked when their waitress stopped by the table. He suggested several dishes and discussed the fresh fish with the woman before ordering. Isa saw the envy in the younger woman's eyes. She twirled the gold band around and around with her thumb.

The evening continued pleasantly enough, rather as if they were polite strangers forced together for a short time. On the way home, she leaned her head back on the headrest and watched the stars. The dreams she'd once had seemed far away.

"I'll drive you down to pick your car up in the morning."

"Okay."

He chuckled with sardonic humor. "Watch it. You're being rather easy tonight. I might ask some impossible task of you while you're in this mood."

She studied his strong profile for a moment. "What

would you ask for if you could have anything your heart desired?''

"A loving family and a happy home," he promptly replied. "My father once told me a man could wish for nothing better."

A piercing sadness gripped her for a moment. He'd mentioned wanting a child and now, a family and home. Harrison wasn't like any man she'd ever known. Her father certainly hadn't cared about his family or whether they had a roof over their heads.

"I'm not asking it of you," he continued in a harder voice. "So don't worry about it."

"I won't." She sat up straight and refused to recognize the hurt his words caused.

Her old car, now officially Rick's since his birthday two weeks ago, wasn't in the garage when they arrived home.

"Did Rick mention he was going out when you left?" she asked, her stomach clenching with the first stirrings of worry.

"No."

Inside, they didn't find a note either on the refrigerator or in his dark, empty room.

At Harrison's black look, she volunteered to wait up for the wayward teenager. The familiar despair surged through her.

"I'll do it. I think it's time he and I had a little talk."

"I'd rather—"

"No."

At his frown, she subsided. "What are you going to do?"

"Ground him, for one thing. I'll think of others as I go along. Don't worry. I won't browbeat him."

"I'll stay up with you."

He shook his head. "A man-to-man talk is called for.

You'd only be in the way. Go on to bed." He went into the study and turned on a light, his expression grim.

She went to their room, but not to sleep. After she was in bed, she lay there and worried.

In a few minutes, Harrison came in, gathered her into his arms without a word and kissed her for a long time. Finally he joined her between the covers when their kisses grew too hot to control. Their lovemaking was wild and terribly sweet.

When she was asleep, Harrison rose silently and dressed. He returned to the den where he waited for his brother-in-law to get home. It was time they had a serious talk.

Rick tried to be extra quiet as he slipped into the house. He hoped Isa hadn't waited up for him.

No such luck. He heard the television in the den. Since he couldn't get to his room without passing the open door, he'd have to face her. Maybe she'd be asleep and wouldn't hear him sneak past. In the morning, he would say he'd been home early.

"Rick? I'd like to see you a minute."

An icy chill raced over his scalp and brought every hair on his head to attention. His luck was the pits, always had been, always would be. He glanced around, then realized there was no escape. Hell, there never was, not for him.

"Get in here." The command was no less firm for being spoken in a deadly quiet tone.

The twin weights of guilt and worry loaded him down as he walked into the den. His brother-in-law turned off the television and motioned for him to have a seat.

Rick sat on the edge of the sofa and leaned forward, arms braced on his knees. He locked his hands together and hoped he looked cool and in control. "Yeah?"

He didn't sound cool, only belligerent and hateful. He didn't know how to talk to someone like Harrison. Isa's husband was really cool, really in control. If he'd had someone like him for a father, maybe things would have been different....

It was too late. The pit was there, waiting for him. His eyes started burning and his throat closed up.

Aww, man. Aww, man. Aww, man.

"I think it's time we came to an understanding."

He glanced up and looked away from the hard stare. He flexed his fingers against each other and kept his gaze on the carpet between his feet.

"Aren't you supposed to be in the house before dark?"

Rick shrugged.

"Your driver's permit is for daytime only, isn't it?"

"Yeah. Yeah, sure." He could feel it coming, the snarly lecture, the sarcastic put-downs, the barbs about him being a stupid kid who didn't know how good he had it. He'd heard them all before...from his dad, the high-school counselor, the guy at the detention center.

"It's almost eleven. The library closed at eight."

He nodded again and waited.

"Give me the keys to the car."

His head snapped up. "What?"

"The keys," Harrison reminded him. "You're grounded for two weeks. From now on, for every time you're late, that'll be a day without wheels."

Rick felt the blood drain away from his face. He almost fainted as relief flooded him. Without wheels, maybe Moe would leave him alone. Maybe he'd drift on somewhere else, find some other sucker to do his dirty work....

"The keys," Harrison repeated. He studied the teenager while the boy dug into his pocket and produced the set of keys.

Harrison took them. Strange, the kid didn't seem especially unhappy at the prospect of being without a car for the last two weeks of school. As a teenager, he'd have been mad as hell, even though it was his own fault.

"Have you anything to say for yourself?" he asked, wanting Rick to open up and talk to him.

"What's to say? You've made up your mind."

The silence twanged like a high-tension wire between them. Harrison nodded as if satisfied. "Are you going to be around to start rebuilding the engine tomorrow?"

The kid didn't look too unhappy, only resigned. His eyes held that same covering mist that Isa's did, disclosing nothing of his inner feelings. "I guess," he muttered.

Harrison tamped down the rising irritation. He heaved a silent breath. "You know," he began conversationally, "I don't give a damn about what happens to you, but your sister happens to care a lot."

The kid's ears turned pink. Talk of his sister got to him. Good. Maybe he had a conscience after all.

"I don't know why. You've done nothing to deserve it, but women are like that," he continued.

That brought a tightening of the big hands that dangled awkwardly between the kid's knees. The boy was going to be large when he finished growing up. It might be harder to straighten him out then.

With a now-or-never grimace, he went on. "I'm going to tell you this one time. Because she's my wife, I'm willing to work things out with you, but you cause any more grief and I'll hand you over to the authorities myself. Is that clear?"

"Yeah."

"So this is the way it's going to be. No drugs. No

missed curfews. No unexplained outings. You getting all this?''

"Yeah, I hear you."

"You'll also apologize to Isa for the worry you've put her through. You have a brain, a damned good one from all I've seen. Use it." Harrison paused, thinking of his dad's lectures from the past. "A man makes his own choices, and he chooses his friends as carefully as he chooses his wife or his car. Isa said you'd been to the casinos with someone. That could get you into real trouble. Ask yourself—is this person being a good friend to you?"

The boy sat silently, his head stubbornly downcast.

"That's it. You'd better get some sleep. We start on the car at eight. Good night."

He watched the lanky youth leap to his feet, his expression one of surprise at being dismissed. "Good night," he mumbled. He loped off toward his room.

Harrison grinned, thinking of his own adolescent days and the relief he'd felt to get out from under his dad's eagle eye and scorching lectures.

Well, they would see how it went. For the kid's sake, he hoped the word had gotten through about the rules of the house.

When he entered the bedroom, he knew at once that Isa was awake. "He's home," he told her.

She raised up on an elbow. "Is he okay?"

"If you mean, did I belt him or something? No. I reminded him of the house rules. I also grounded him for two weeks." He laid the car keys on the tray on the dresser along with his change, comb and wallet. "He'll have to ride the bus, or I'll give him a lift to school in the mornings. You can pick him up if you wish."

"I will." There was a long pause. "Thank you, Harrison."

One thing he'd learned about her—his sweet blackmailer could be gracious, at least where her brother was concerned.

He shucked his clothes and got into bed. After turning out the lamp, he hesitated, then gave in to temptation and pulled her into his arms.

She was still a mystery to him—this wildly passionate woman who set his blood on fire, this keen-minded con artist who could play poker like a man, this wily female who had blackmailed him into giving her his name and a year out of his life—but neither passion nor cunning would outsmart him. He wasn't sure what the stakes were between them, but he would win, whatever the cost.

Chapter Eleven

"Lunch," Isa called to her brother and husband.

They were bent over the old car she'd bought secondhand. Parts lay in an orderly row on a flattened cardboard box over in the corner of the garage. This was the second weekend they'd worked on the project.

"Are you sure you know where those parts go?" she demanded, setting plates of sandwiches and chips on a workbench. Laughter bubbled out of her when the two men straightened. "Now I know how the term 'grease monkey' came into use."

"Go ahead, laugh," Harrison told her. "We're saving you a bundle of money on this bucket of bolts."

"Yeah, and you're getting a first-class job," Rick put in.

Still laughing, she went inside for drinks while they cleaned up. She returned with her plate and three glasses of Maggie's spiced tea on a tray. They sat in the shade and ate.

"It's hot today," Rick commented, wiping the sweat off on the sleeve of his T-shirt.

"Ninety-two, according to the thermometer by the pool."

"You been for a swim?" Harrison gazed at her shorts and halter with that lazy sensuality that still caused jolts of electricity to run over her.

"No, I thought I'd wait for you guys to join me. Are you going to finish up soon?"

They'd worked on the car from dawn until dark last weekend. She didn't really expect this one to be any different. She sighed, not realizing she had until she saw Harrison observing her. She smiled.

"Bored?" he asked.

She shook her head. "Not really. Not exactly," she corrected, trying to be truthful. "It's just that I've never sat around before. I mean, I've always worked."

"Yeah," Rick agreed, "usually two jobs."

Remorse stung her. "I was never there for you." She sighed again. "There were so many bills—" She shut up. She didn't want to come across as a poor-me person.

Harrison caught every nuance in her words. More and more, she felt cornered by him, like a small critter under the eye of a predator. She wished he didn't make her feel so vulnerable. She'd never had this problem before. She had to be strong for Rick. But sometimes, lying in her husband's arms, she thought of how it would be to have someone to share life and its problems...for always.

Pain coursed through her. It came more frequently of late. She stared at the distant vista until she drove it away. She couldn't afford to think beyond the year. Blackmailers couldn't plan further than the next scam. For her, there wouldn't be another one.

When her marriage and sojourn here were over, she

and Rick would move on to greener pastures, so to speak. She gazed at the sparse landscape. She'd miss the desert when they left.

"The desert has a beauty all its own, doesn't it?" Harrison murmured, his gaze following hers.

She nodded.

"It's neat," Rick put in after polishing off his sandwich. He took a gulp of tea. "I didn't think I'd like it, but the other day, my biology class went on a hike. There's a lot of wildlife out here, things I'd never have thought of looking for."

"We have hawks and eagles in these parts." Harrison pointed out an eagle riding an air current along the ridge behind the house. "Once, on a foggy day, I saw a raptor sitting on nearly every fence post."

"What's a raptor?" Isa asked.

"Birds of prey," Rick explained. "We're studying the balance of life in the area. Raptors are important because without them the rodents would soon overrun the place."

Isa listened while her brother expounded on nature. She wondered if that was his calling—a wildlife biologist. Her eyes met Harrison's, and she knew he was thinking the same. It was a moment of perfect accord.

The blue in his eyes deepened as his gaze warmed. She recalled waking early that morning to his rapturous kisses.

A blush worked its way into her face, although she tried hard to hold it in. His smile, though sardonic, widened as if he could read her thoughts, and she had to look away. When they made love, she couldn't control her feelings. He made her wild with passion and the delight she found in his arms.

It would be easy to fall in love—

No. She wouldn't. That would be stupid. In less than

a year, she'd pack up and leave him to his life. Rick would be put into her custody permanently. They would be happy.

A loving family. A happy home.

No, she couldn't think about that. It would be hard enough to leave here....

"How would you like to work for me?" Harrison asked.

She darted a quick glance at him. He was looking at her.

"I'd like to," Rick said before she could reply.

"Sorry, I don't have an opening for a broker with your qualifications," Harrison said. "However, there's an import company in the building. They need somebody on the loading dock. The pay is decent. Interested?"

"Sure. What do I do to get it?"

"Drop by Monday and put in an application. We should have the jalopy up and running this weekend, maybe today...if we can get on with the work without unnecessary distractions." His glance slid to her.

"If you're finished with lunch, I will take myself off," she declaimed, nose in the air. "I certainly wouldn't want to be accused of distracting men from their work."

Harrison handed her his plate, then cupped the back of her neck and pulled her to him for a rousing kiss. "There," he murmured, "maybe that'll take the edge off your sharp tongue."

Rick ducked his head back under the hood as if embarrassed by their display, but he wore a wide grin.

"Do *you* want a job?" Harrison asked Isa. "The hours are long, the pay is lousy and you have to sleep with the boss."

"Seriously?"

"Cross my heart."

Thrills chased over her at the thought of working with her handsome husband every day. "Yes, I'd like to try it."

"Good. You want to go in with me Monday morning?"

She nodded. "After a week of lazing around, I'm ready to try anything."

"Thanks," he said dryly.

"I'm sure I'll enjoy the experience."

"This'll be something else you can add to your résumé." He picked up a screwdriver and one of the parts neatly lined up on the cardboard. "Business manager, restaurant hostess, temporary office help, baby-sitter, temptress…"

She froze in place and waited for his next term.

"Wife," he drawled, his eyes on her.

Relieved that he'd left out blackmailer—Rick didn't know about that—she gathered the dishes and went inside. After rinsing and putting the used plates away, she retrieved the pitcher of iced tea from the refrigerator.

An attack of nerves hit her as she thought of working in the same office as her husband. She hastily set the pitcher on the counter. Perhaps it was a mistake to let their lives become more entangled. That would make it harder to leave.

She folded her arms across her waist and stared at the sage-covered hills, fighting the inner turmoil.

Wanting things—this job, this house, this person— only led to grief. She'd learned that long ago. She held herself tightly in check until the longing passed. A lingering sadness remained.

Isa smiled and repeated the name of each person she met. Adele was Harrison's gorgon of a secretary, as he'd called her at the mountain cabin.

The woman didn't fit Isa's image of a gorgon at all. She was petite and shapely and maybe thirty years old. Her pleated skirt needed another three inches to reach her knees, her blouse dipped rather low between her breasts and her streaky blond hair had that tousled, just-out-of-bed look that men fell for.

Jealousy was not a pretty emotion, Isa reminded herself. She smiled and smiled during the introductions.

Someone had brought doughnuts in. The whole group—seventeen people counting her husband, his secretary, Ken the financial whiz, James Riley Parker, the third officer, with Harrison and Ken, of the corporation, the three typists who kept track of things for the men and ten others who were managers of production, marketing, and various tasks—lingered over coffee and doughnuts in the executive offices.

She and Harrison did, too. Thirty minutes passed in pleasant chitchat and speculative glances.

"Okay," her husband finally said. "Come on. I'll get you started, then Ken can take over. He likes to train people to his way of doing things."

"Because my way is logical," Ken spoke up. "Harrison's isn't," he added in a loud aside to Isa.

She laughed and relaxed somewhat.

Inside his office, Harrison closed the door and motioned her to a chair beside his desk. She noticed he'd placed his desk so he could look out the windows.

"You can see our...your house," she exclaimed in surprise.

"Our house," he corrected in a voice like chipped stone. "We are married. We do live there together."

Before she had time to react, he'd taken his seat. She didn't know what had made him angry.

"I'll explain the various departments and the pecking order." As he talked, he became warmer. It was obvious he liked his employees and was proud of the company. Once he laughed, a happy, carefree sound that enchanted her.

It would be so easy to think this could last. The sadness that gripped her at unexpected moments of late wrapped around her heart. With it came the longing.

She wanted…she couldn't put a name to it. Something wild and wonderful, something that would last, something, she realized, that Harrison would share with the woman he ultimately fell in love with.

That woman wouldn't be her.

"I need you to take over some of the marketing accounts. The manager retired recently. He worked for my father. The department is about thirty years behind the times. I want you to bring it up-to-date."

"How up-to-date do you want to get?"

"Twenty-first century."

"There're some very good marketing packages on the shelf these days. What kind of computer system do you have?"

He gave her a lopsided grin.

Her mouth dropped open. "None?"

"Well, they do have one in the department. I think you have to crank it to get it started."

"Do we have a budget for equipment?"

"Yes, thanks to Zeke Merry."

The name stilled the conversation and brought back memories of the weekend in Tahoe. "I liked him," she finally said.

"Me, too. He isn't bad for a partner. So far, he's letting my team run things."

"A wise man," she murmured.

Harrison leaned forward, elbows on the desk, and

gazed into her eyes. "Thanks for the vote of confidence."

The intensity flustered her. "You're quite welcome." She'd sounded as prim as a spinster. Harrison chuckled.

Isa found she liked making her dynamic husband laugh. When he assigned her to Ken to learn the ropes and told her he'd see her at five, she hurried out of the office.

By the time noon rolled around, Isa was ready to call it a day. Her head was stuffed with terms and conditions and caveats she must watch for in the accounts she would handle.

Over lunch, Ken told her about the oversupply brokerage business Harrison had started on his own before he'd had to take over the family enterprises. Ken had worked for him.

"What exactly does an oversupply broker do?" she asked.

"We contract to find a buyer for manufacturing overruns or cancelled orders. That way, the manufacturer recovers all or part of his costs, the customer gets a good deal and we make a percentage of the proceeds. Everyone is happy."

"Harrison started it on his own?"

"Yeah. He's smart that way. Some of the tricks the manufacturing reps pulled were unbelievable," he explained. "Such as dumping ten thousand billiard balls on us at one time. The balls were warped and veered off at odd angles when rolled. The buyer refused to take the shipment."

"What happened?"

"Harrison had the manufacturer coat 'em with soft rubber to make them safe for kids and sold them to a chain of toy stores as goofballs. They were a sensation one Christmas.''

"Ah, a brilliant idea.''

"Yeah. Harrison has all the luck.''

Ken's appreciative perusal startled her. She covered her surprise with a quip. "He might not agree.''

"I think he would. His marriage fits right in his usual mode of operation.''

"How's that?'' She smiled blandly, but she loved the chance to learn more about her husband.

"Drop a silver dollar and pick up a gold piece.''

She tried to figure out what that meant.

"He was dating someone,'' Ken elaborated, "from among the county's top families, a divorcée who planned to make him husband number three, I think. He found you instead. Lucky man.''

Isa's innate honesty wouldn't let her accept Ken's view. "He didn't exactly find me. I came here planning on blackmailing him into marriage by whatever means necessary. You must have realized that up at Tahoe.''

"Yeah. Like I said, Harrison has incredible luck.''

Harrison's friend thought their marriage was a good thing. She sighed in relief. For some reason, that made her feel not quite so deceitful.

Maybe at the end of the year, Harrison would want her to stay. Maybe he'd beg her to continue the marriage, to live with him forever.

Maybe pigs would fly....

"Now I'll take you to the guy you'll be working with. James Riley Parker III is the vice president and has been with the company since the mine began commercial operations.''

"This Mr. Parker, he knew Harrison's father?''

"Yeah, they go way back. He's a grouch, so pay no attention to his sour face.''

Isa clenched her hands as excitement gripped her. Maybe he knew about her father and the silver mine. Maybe she could prove to Harrison she had a right in his life.

Mr. Parker turned out to be a formidable old bear who looked on the world—her included—in disapproval. He set her to going through contracts and invoices for the past year. She saw he'd sold a shipment of costume jewelry to a chain of department stores to use as gifts to celebrate the parent company's one hundredth birthday.

"This was brilliant," she exclaimed to her mentor.

He growled at her. She got back to work.

At five, Harrison rescued her. "How was your first day?" he asked on the ride to the house.

"Tiring. My brain is on overload."

He laughed.

She snuggled down in the seat, content for the moment.

"Are you going to sleep on me?" he asked. "I got worried the last time you did that."

"The day we went to the judge's office and got Rick," she mused. "I don't know what came over me. I couldn't stay awake."

"Stress will do that."

She fidgeted with her wedding band. "You've been more than kind to Rick. He's different lately...since you two worked on the car. I think he needed a male to relate to."

"Ah, yes, you approve of me as a role model."

"I do." She injected as much sincerity as she could into the words. "I appreciate your not letting the situation between us interfere in your dealings with him."

He lifted her hand and kissed it. "Sometimes the situation between us is pretty damn good." The sensuous deepening of his voice and the promise in his eyes when he flicked her a glance recalled the passion between them.

She wanted to ask him about the woman he'd dated and how serious it had been and to tell him she was sorry for interfering in his life. However, she didn't. She couldn't take back what had happened, but she would uphold her end of the bargain.

Isa set the vase of flowers at the end of the hall table, then flicked a hand over its pristine surface. She moved a crystal bowl of potpourri an inch one way, then back.

The Fourth of July party was about to begin. This time the gala was for Harrison's friends.

Hearing a car engine in the drive, she drew a deep breath and checked her appearance in the mirror over the table. She wore a bright cotton beach dress over her swimsuit. Instead of shoes, she'd stretched a band of silk flowers around her ankle and over her toes.

When no one came to the front door, she peered out to see what was keeping them. The car was empty.

Hearing voices in the back, she realized the guests knew to go directly to the pool. She hurried from the entrance to the back patio.

"Here, take these chips," Maggie ordered as Isa hurried through the kitchen.

She stepped outside carrying a basket lined with a red napkin and filled with blue and yellow corn chips. In her other hand, she held a lazy Susan with bowls of salsa and dips.

"There's my wife," Harrison said to the three guests. "Isa, come meet some friends from my youth."

"Your wild and wicked youth," the sultry-voiced woman standing close to him teased. She had black hair and dark, flashing eyes, crimson lips and a seductive smile.

Isa felt a stiffening along her spine. She put on her company smile and went to them. Harrison stepped forward and threw an arm over her shoulders, tucking her into his side.

"Honey, this is Helen," he introduced them. "And the Murrays. We grew up in these parts."

She didn't catch the couple's first names or any of the conversation about the weather that followed. Helen, his old friend—the divorcée who'd planned on making him husband number three?—was the most strikingly beautiful woman Isa had ever seen. She could barely refrain from staring.

Helen had a perfect oval face, large soulful eyes, an alabaster complexion with a hint of duskiness to it. Taken separately, each feature was perfect. Together, they formed a portrait of delicate refinement. The skillful use of makeup only enhanced the whole.

"Darling, you should have told us of your marriage," Helen chided Harrison with a pretty pout. "We would have held a reception for you."

"That's what I was afraid of."

Helen patted him on the arm. "He always hated formal outings. You'd have thought he was going to a hanging when his parents insisted he come to my birthday parties," she explained to Isa with a reproachful glance at Harrison.

Isa wasn't sure people had hackles, but if they did, hers were raised to their highest point. When Harrison released her to check on the slabs of ribs cooking on the grill, she retreated to the house.

"Was that Helen?" Maggie asked. She leaned over the counter to peer outside, but the potted plants hid the others from view.

"Yes," Isa said. "Also a couple...the Murrays, I think."

"Oh, yes, Phil and Flo. Harrison, Phil and Helen were inseparable while they were growing up. Helen is Phil's cousin. Her parents were killed during a break-in at their house and Phil's family took her in. She was an heiress as well as having looks, so the boys were always after her."

"Poor little rich girl," Isa murmured, and was immediately ashamed of the remark.

"Except for Harrison," Maggie mused, apparently not hearing the muttering from the green-eyed monster Isa felt herself to be. "He never paid much attention to girls before going off to college. I think Helen had an eye for him, but he didn't see her that way. I guess she was more like a sister."

"Hah," Isa mumbled, setting glasses on a tray.

"I'll have the hot stuff ready in about ten minutes. Did you take the vegetable tray out?"

"Not yet."

"Take the glasses. I'll bring the rest. Remind your husband to serve the champagne. He tends to forget."

Isa marched outside with the glasses and herself in hand. She was not a jealous person, never had been, wasn't going to be. So that was that.

Her resolution lasted all of ten seconds. That was when she rounded the potted patio tree and saw Helen press herself against Harrison. She kissed his cheek.

When she saw Isa watching them, she called out gaily, "Don't be jealous. I was congratulating Harrison on his good taste. He said your anniversary is tomorrow. All this time and not a word from him to his oldest friends. I'm hurt."

The other couple had moved off and were talking to other guests who had arrived, Isa saw. She placed the tray of glasses on the refreshment table set in the shade along one wall.

"Has it been three months?" Harrison asked. "Let's see, we married in April. May, June, July. Yep, tomorrow is three months of married bliss."

He saw his wife slip into her gracious-hostess mode, her smile lovely, her every thought hidden. Only he knew how radiant her smile could be in unguarded moments. Only he knew how she responded to every caress of his with one of her own. He liked being the one person there who knew her so thoroughly.

Slowly but surely, he was peeling back the layers and discovering the real person. He stifled his impatience. At the end of their year, he'd know her completely. A dangerous recklessness swept over him. He'd know her. Or else.

"I'll serve the drinks," he told Isa, moving away from Helen. She reminded him of a strangler fig, wrapping herself around a man until he was in danger of being smothered.

At least he didn't have that problem with his wife. In fact, he sometimes wished she would cling a bit. Hmm, maybe he could make her jealous.... No, that would be a cheap shot.

"Would you ask Rick to come take care of the ribs for a few minutes? He said he'd help with the cooking."

Isa blinked in surprise. Rick, cooking? She went to his bedroom. He was reading and tapping his foot to the music audible to him through the earphones he wore.

He and Harrison had grown increasingly close during the past month. They'd gone fishing one weekend, camping out in the mountains and hiking through the woods. Man stuff, Harrison had told her with a superior air.

"Yeah," Rick had echoed, a big happy grin on his face.

She was glad they were getting along. She wrinkled her nose. She was also a little jealous of their friendship. Her own relationship with her husband was hard to define.

"Harrison says he needs help with the ribs," she told her brother when he removed the earpieces.

"Be right with you." He jumped up, turned off the music and headed down the hall with her.

Isa thought he'd grown taller. He looked healthy and fit since he'd started working in shipping and receiving at the import warehouse after school let out for the summer. He stood straighter. His step was confident, his stride assured. Like Harrison's.

Her baby brother was opening up, too. One day she'd come home at noon to find Maggie and Rick dancing in the kitchen. She'd been stunned by his happy laughter as Maggie showed him an intricate step.

If only it could last.

Nine more months. Time enough for a child. A painful constriction knotted her throat. Harrison hadn't mentioned having a baby again. She thought of it sometimes. She'd loved rocking and singing to her brother when he was a baby.

When they reached the patio, Harrison beckoned Rick to the barbecue pit and told him what to do. Rick took over. Harrison removed champagne from a cooler filled with ice, beer and cola. She noticed that Helen stayed by his side.

After a couple of minutes, Isa began to fume. Not only was the other woman sticking to Harrison like flypaper, but she was acting as his hostess by welcoming the guests, pointing out the refreshment table and holding the glasses while Harrison poured.

Maggie came to the door and motioned for Isa to help her. When she went inside, Maggie had the hot snacks ready.

"Here, serve these before they get cold. These are Ken's favorites," she added before Isa could respond. She thrust the platter into Isa's hands, turned her around with hands on her shoulders and muttered close to her ear, "Go get 'em, girl. Don't let that witch take your place." She gave her a push.

Isa marched to the patio and joined her husband, his old friend and the financial whiz.

"Ken, hello," she said, injecting honeyed warmth into her voice. "Maggie said these were your favorite snacks, so I'm giving you first go at them."

"Ah, that Maggie, a girl after my own heart...right after you." He winked, then selected a chimichanga from the tray.

"Do you want champagne or beer? The beer is in the cooler," Isa advised before Helen could butt in.

"Maggie's spiced tea is the drink of choice for us nerds. I'll take some of that."

"It's in the pitcher on the end of the table. Ice cubes in the bucket behind it. Help yourself."

Isa turned to Harrison. "Who's next?"

"James Riley. I haven't greeted him yet."

She saw the old curmudgeon talking to the couple who'd arrived with Helen. Mr. Parker had let her handle her first sale last week. He'd told her the range of prices she could work with, then had hovered over her during the entire transaction while she and the buyer for the other company haggled.

When the deal was done, she'd turned to him, excited at getting near the top mark for the shipment of earrings she'd sold to a chain of mall jewelry kiosks. Mr. Parker had grunted and gone back to his office without a word.

"If he ever smiled, his face would crack," she'd complained to Harrison on the way home that night.

"I felt the same when he was helping me come on board. He always told me what I was doing wrong, but he never mentioned it when I did right."

"Exactly," Isa had said.

She smiled as she and Harrison went together to greet the old man. "I'm so glad you could come," she said after they'd said hello. "That's a lovely shirt."

"Thank you."

Mr. Parker wore dress slacks, but he'd left off his tie and jacket in favor of a tropical dress shirt of white cotton with an embroidered vine motif along the front.

"My wife was Filipino and quite skillful with the needle. She made me a dozen shirts before she passed on so I'd have enough to last my lifetime."

"How thoughtful," Isa murmured, unable to think of another word to say. She realized her grumpy mentor had at least one soft spot in him.

Harrison met her eyes. His gaze was lambent. For a second, she was filled with longing for things she couldn't have. It made her angry with herself, and with him. Sexy or sardonic she could handle. She didn't want anything else between them.

After all their guests had arrived, Harrison went to help Rick with the ribs. Isa replenished the platters of snacks and checked with Maggie on the vegetables that went with the meat.

"Everything is under control," Maggie assured her. She hummed along with a country-western song coming from a portable radio on the kitchen counter while she peeked at the ears of corn roasting in the oven. "Go. Go on," Maggie shooed her from the kitchen. "Have fun. It's your party."

Like a bashful child, Isa drifted outside. Thirty people, half of them couples, milled around the area. Five guys, including her husband, were in the pool playing water polo. Several women sat on the side, dangling their legs in the water.

Helen relaxed on a chaise longue under an umbrella, sipping a glass of champagne and chatting with Flo Murray and another woman. She'd removed her silk wraparound. Her body was lean and tanned, very fit.

Isa was surprised the woman wasn't in the pool with the men, showing off her Olympic swimming skills or some such.

She put aside the catty thought when she noticed Mr. Parker sitting alone in the shade. After a second's hesitation, she walked across the patio. There were things she wanted to ask him about the past. She joined him.

"Nice party," he said with much more cordiality than he'd ever shown at the office.

"Thank you."

"I was surprised when the boy married."

She grinned when he nodded toward Harrison. She'd thought of many descriptive terms for her husband, including stubborn and mulish, but she'd never thought of him as a boy.

"But I was glad of it," Mr. Parker continued, his tone serious. "A man needs a wife to add joy to his life."

Isa had a sudden sense of his loneliness. It touched her, bringing the tightening to her throat again. She'd never been prone to tears, but during the three months of her marriage, she'd often had to hold them in. Sometimes when Harrison made exquisite love to her, she couldn't. It was as if she mourned her marriage before it was over.

"Hello, you two. What secrets are you telling, stuck away over here by yourselves?" Helen demanded.

Isa tamped down her irritation.

"We were agreeing that wives are the great civilizing influences in the world," Mr. Parker said. He gave a sly grin that made him look like a devious cherub, albeit a bald one.

Helen's smile became brittle. "Yes. Several of us were wondering how anyone ever managed to get Harrison to the altar. He's been a determined bachelor for years."

"It was an impulse." Isa felt her ears grow hot, and wished she didn't blush when she lied.

"I must confess to being fascinated by anyone who could catch him. You were an actress before you moved here, weren't you? Back in Oregon? A bit player, I heard."

Ah, the woman had been doing some checking on her. "I did a few parts, yes, but my degree is in business. I was an assistant manager."

"She's got a head on her shoulders," Mr. Parker said as if she were his personal protégé.

Helen ignored him. "What was your maiden name? I may have seen you in Ashland. I visited friends there last summer."

"Chavez. Isadora Chavez is my name."

Helen considered. "No, I don't remember it." She studied Isa with a doubtful expression.

Isa wondered if the woman thought she was lying about her past. Why would she? Her life was an open book. Except for the deception involving her marriage. She'd had to do that. She'd had to have a home for Rick.

She glanced around the patio and at the country surrounding the house. This home was a good place for a boy to grow to manhood. Harrison was wonderful and kind and...

The longing hit her, harder this time. She swallowed hard to control it. A person couldn't go around getting choked up all the time. She saw Mr. Parker studying her curiously and managed a smile, once more in control.

When the food was served, Helen left to join her cousin and his wife as they lined up for the lavish meal. Isa breathed a sigh of relief. She and Helen weren't going to be bosom buddies.

"Chavez," Mr. Parker mused. "I once knew a fellow by that name. It was years ago, though."

Isa's hands went cold and clammy. "It's a common Hispanic name, like Smith or Jones in English. Was this man a friend?"

He snorted in contempt. "Not mine. He was a partner to the boy's father. They'd taken claim to an old silver mine that everyone assumed was played out. They found a new lode, though, and started it up again. It was a small operation, just the two of them trying to scrape together enough cash for equipment."

"What happened to them?"

"Dan Stone was always having to bail Chavez out of trouble. The man was a drinker and a gambler, a loser in every way."

Isa's face burned at this assessment of her father. It was true, but that didn't make it any easier to hear.

"He got in over his head in an illegal gambling operation," Mr. Parker confided. "Dan scraped together enough money to pay off the debt, but he'd had it by then. He made Chavez put up his interest in the mine as collateral. Chavez lit out one day and left Dan with another pile of unpaid bills that had been charged to the mine. We never saw him again, but Dan heard the man had married some woman over near the coast and had a baby a few years later. He used to worry about them. I say it was a case of good riddance myself.''

Isa swallowed hard. "Yes, I think you're right.''

"The food is ready. We'd better get in line before it's gone.'' He chuckled at his joke.

"You go ahead. I need to help Maggie.'' Isa retreated to the master bedroom and closed the door.

She sat on the side of the luxurious tub, which she and Harrison hadn't yet used, and watched the laughing people on the patio. Harrison was forking racks of the succulent ribs onto his guests' plates. Rick, wearing an oven mitt, put a foil-wrapped baked potato beside the meat. Maggie set platters of corn and vegetables on the refreshment table.

The scene blurred as Isa pondered the conversation with Mr. Parker. He had unknowingly given her the key to her past.

That woman had been her mother. She had been that baby.

Her father had lied. The mining claim she'd self-righteously staked her and Rick's future on wasn't worth a cent. She and Rick had no right to anything that belonged to Harrison Stone, no right at all.

Chapter Twelve

Isa stood at the window and watched the movement of trucks and workers along the street. The building, located in an area of small manufacturing businesses and their related warehouses, housed a wholesale import business on the first floor, the jewelry-making business on the second floor and Harrison's corporate offices on the third.

She could see her brother sitting on the loading dock three stories down from her. He was eating his lunch, his back against the wall, one leg dangling over the edge of the dock.

Worry ate at her like an invasion of locusts, nibbling constantly at the edges of her mind. God help her, she didn't know what to do.

Her conscience didn't help at all. It merely yelled at her like an irate parent, reminding her she was living a lie, that she'd forced Harrison into marriage without just cause, that she and Rick weren't entitled to one cent from the mine even if it had been turning a profit.

The jewelry business was the only lucrative part of Stone Enterprises. Her family wasn't entitled to any part of it, since it had been started by Daniel Stone long after her father had run off and left Stone with a mound of debts.

She ran a hand through her hair and felt the tight, stressed muscles in her neck and back. She'd had a headache for most of the week after talking to Mr. Parker on the weekend.

A bone-weary sigh escaped her.

"Tired?" a voice asked from behind her.

She jerked around. Harrison stood in the doorway. Her heart gave a hitch, then beat very fast. She forced a smile that felt more like a grimace.

"Somewhat," she said lightly. "This wheeling and dealing is hard work. I think I'd rather stick to updating the accounting department. Computers may have minds of their own, but they don't talk back."

"Have you had lunch?"

She looked at a empty soda can and the remains of a peanut-butter-and-cracker package from the candy machine on her desk. "Uh, I wasn't very hungry."

"That wasn't a proper meal. The gals go out to lunch one Friday a month. Today was the day. Did anyone invite you?" He walked around the desk and stopped beside her.

"Yes, but I declined. I thought I'd be a damper."

"Being the boss's wife?"

"Yes." She was engulfed by all the things she'd come to associate with her virile husband—his warmth and strength, the scent of his aftershave and talc, his masculine presence that thrilled and excited her.

She'd miss him when she was gone.

Harrison turned her and began to massage her shoulders. He could feel the tension vibrating through her like electrical impulses through a wire. She lived on the edge. Whatever bothered her, she kept it to herself.

However, there was one part of her he knew as well as he knew himself. Her passion. She couldn't hide her body's response to him. When they came together, she was as fervid in her hunger for him as he was for her. It was the one thing that dispelled his anger at being trapped.

He rubbed the taut cords running up her neck to her skull. She bent her head forward to give him better access. He heard her sigh. Unable to resist, he lifted the heavy fall of hair and kissed her neck.

Her fragrance filled his nostrils and made him wish they were home. Only in bed did they communicate without shadows and subterfuge between them. At least they had, until this week.

After the party last weekend, Isa had withdrawn even further behind her composed smile. At night, when they made love, he could sense her holding part of herself aloof, even though she reacted with satisfying vigor.

He rubbed most of the tension out, then slipped his arms around her narrow waist and hugged her to him.

"You've been quiet this week," he murmured against her temple. "Did Helen say something to hurt you last weekend?"

The tension returned. "No, of course not."

He tightened his arms in regret. "I wish she weren't part of my past. Getting mixed up with her, even for a short time, was a mistake. I realized it and got out before I got stuck in her web, thank God."

"Instead, you got stuck in mine."

He could read nothing in her tone, other than the

touch of irony she often injected into her discussions with him.

"It hasn't been all bad." He realized that much was true. "Sometimes the reward is worth the risk." He kissed her neck again, then lingered to trace his tongue over the smooth skin. His body reacted as usual.

A shiver flowed through her.

An answering tremor hit him. Everything about her excited him in a way no woman ever had. It angered him, but he couldn't escape it. However, he had a piece of business to discuss with her at this moment. He suppressed the desire.

"I talked to Harry this morning," he murmured against her temple. "He's researched the mining claim."

"What...what did he find out?"

"Nothing directly. There was flooding in a basement where some of the early records were stored. Several boxes were destroyed. There's no record of an earlier claim. My father filed again, but in his name alone the second time. I don't know why."

I do. Isa gulped the words down before they could spring from her mouth. Guilt gnawed at her.

"If your claim is valid, then..." Harrison sounded baffled, uncertain about his father's actions.

She bit her bottom lip until it hurt. She'd put the doubts in his mind. Her family's claim, discharged long ago by Dan Stone, had forced the son to consider that his parent had acted less than honorably in the past. He'd hate her when he found out the truth.

Staring out the window, Harrison's breath soft on her skin, she wished she could vanish in a puff of smoke like a genie into a bottle and wipe all memory of her from his mind.

Since she couldn't simply disappear from his life, she

knew she should tell him the truth before he found out from someone else who, like Mr. Parker, had known his father and hers.

Tell him. Tell him now, her conscience urged.

"Who's that with Rick?" Harrison asked.

Isa released the pressure on her lip and looked to where Harrison pointed. Another young man stood close to her brother. They were engrossed in conversation, an angry one if she was reading their body language accurately.

"He looks familiar," she said, "something about the way he moves, but I can't see his face."

"A friend from school?"

"I don't know."

Rick had been happy lately. He walked with his head up and his shoulders back, a bounce in his step. She'd heard him whistling while he worked in the yard or cleaned the pool, two jobs that Harrison had assigned to the younger man.

He also received a healthy allowance plus a list of extras he could do to earn money if the chores were warranted. Harrison didn't believe in busywork or pay for nothing. Rick was becoming the responsible, dependable person she'd known he could be, given half a chance. They were growing close again.

"Looks as if they're in a disagreement over something."

"Yes." A frisson of worry swept over her. She brushed it aside. "It's probably nothing. Teenagers are prone to take things to heart...." She trailed off, thinking of the state of her own unstable organ.

"Do you?" Harrison asked. He nuzzled on her ear.

Heat formed inside her. Only when he touched her could she forget her troubles, but that wouldn't work forever. She had to face things sooner or later.

She stalled for time. "Sometimes."

"Like us? Like this?" he probed. His tongue circled the rim of her ear before he settled to nibbling on the lobe.

She'd been aware of the need he didn't bother to hide from the moment he'd cuddled her against him. It awakened the hunger in her. With it came the desires of the heart that she could no longer deny. She wished that Harrison would want to keep them, her and her brother. She wished he could learn to love them as they were learning to love and trust him. Oh, God, she wished...

He released her and locked the door to her office. When he came back to her, she was watching him in wide-eyed surprise.

"Surely it doesn't come as a shock that a husband might want his beautiful wife other than when they're at home in bed." He fixed the blinds so that no one could see into the office.

His smile was slow and lazy, his gaze intent when he began to undress. Her hand flew to her throat, which still had a tendency to clog up with emotion when she saw him unclothed.

"You next," he murmured. He reached for her suit jacket, then paused, a question in his eyes.

"If someone should come," she whispered, glancing anxiously at the door. A sexy grin spread over his face. A blush ran over hers.

"Everyone is out to lunch," he assured her.

"But if they aren't. I mean, what would they think..."

"That we want to be alone," he whispered. He slipped the jacket from her, then her blouse and skirt and shoes. He kissed the various parts of her as they were exposed.

At last, he sat her on the desk, the smooth paper of

the desk pad cool under her bare skin. He meandered around her neck, lingered at her breasts, then moved down to her thighs, leaving a trail of wet kisses in his path.

She closed her eyes and moaned as need overrode good sense. She made one last attempt at sanity. "Harrison, we shouldn't."

"We should. It's the only time we're totally open with each other." He nudged her legs farther apart.

Heat engulfed her, spreading slowly from deep inside as he pleasured her until she went mindless from his touch. She stroked through his hair as endless waves of delight broke over her, making her whimper. He gave a low growl and continued his attentions to her.

She called his name urgently. When she convulsed, he rose and entered her, thrusting to the very center. He absorbed her muted cries with his mouth as they both experienced the shattering bliss together. Afterward, she slumped against him, too weary to move.

He held her for a long time, his hands gentle as he rubbed her back from shoulders to hips.

"I didn't mean to go this far. I didn't have anything with me," he said. "Do you think we started a baby?"

"I...I don't know." She stirred and lifted her head, knowing it was time to rejoin reality. "Probably not."

He heaved a deep breath. "Not quite nine months."

She looked away from his searching gaze. "Yes."

"The year is up in April, but school isn't out until the middle of June. There's still time."

"I could never give a child up." She choked on the words and shook her head helplessly.

"Neither could I." He handed her clothing to her. They dressed in silence.

"What would happen if I were pregnant?" she asked.

"We'd have to come to a new agreement, I suppose.'' He gave her a probing look, his eyes dark and moody, a challenge in them that she couldn't decipher.

She looked away.

''We don't have to worry about that until it happens,'' he said as if tired of the conversation. Pulling his suit jacket on, he walked out.

After raising the blinds, she opened the window and let the one-hundred-and-ten-degree heat sweep into the office, driving out the scent of their lovemaking and the questions she couldn't answer and that he wouldn't.

When she looked into the parking area behind the building, she saw Rick unloading boxes from a truck. His boss came out and gave him some instructions, then headed back into the air-conditioned interior. Rick continued to work alone, a lanky, earnest adolescent growing to manhood.

Her heart constricted with love for him. He really was trying to turn over a new leaf, thanks to Harrison's influence. That was almost enough to justify her continuing the lie.

Almost.

But sooner or later she would have to tell Harrison that his father hadn't cheated hers when Dan Stone had refiled the claim in his name only. She should do it before he found out from someone else. With the attorney investigating the claim, it could only be a matter of time....

She clasped her arms across her waist and wondered if Harrison would let Rick stay and finish this year of school. She would have to leave, of course, but if he'd let Rick stay, she would have time to find a job and establish a home for them.

It was the most she would let herself hope for.

* * *

"Maggie?"

Rick waited until Maggie looked up from the dinner salad she was putting together.

"What is it?" she asked.

"Nothing."

"Huh." She went back to work.

He twiddled with a straw. He'd stopped at a fast-food drive-through and picked up a cola on the way here. His boss had sent him home as soon as the truck was unloaded and the stuff stacked in the storage room. It was too hot to do any more today. Rick was to come in early in the morning to finish.

"Uh…"

Maggie glanced up again.

"Nothing," he said.

She put the salad in the fridge, poured a glass of iced tea and fanned herself with a folded piece of paper. At a hundred and ten degrees, even the air-conditioning was hard put to keep the house cool. They'd had salads or sandwiches for dinner every night that week. Too hot to cook.

"What's bothering you, kid?"

He liked that about Maggie. She had a bite, but she was upfront with a person. Could he tell her about Moe? God, he had to tell somebody or go crazy.

"If…if you knew somebody…and they were going to do something like, crooked, you know?"

"Uh-huh."

"What would you do?"

"How crooked? How good a friend?"

Maggie dove right to the heart of a matter. She understood things. Isa would have told him he had to turn them in to the police and given him a lecture about honor and all that. This was more complicated.

"Not much of a friend," he admitted. He slurped up the last of the soda. It made a loud noise in the quiet kitchen, a kid's noise. He pushed the empty cup away and propped his elbows on the counter.

"Can you turn him in?" she asked.

He shook his head. "He hasn't done anything yet."

"What's he gonna do?"

Rick swallowed but it didn't dislodge the lump in his throat. He cast a furtive glance around the kitchen, the living room. This was his home now. He loved it here. He wanted to stay. Moe could ruin everything.

Misery burned his throat. *Aww, man.*

"Well, uh, rob a place."

"What's he want you to do?"

Yeah, Maggie understood. "Leave the loading-bay door unlocked tomorrow when I'm through."

"Uh-huh," she said with a knowing twist. "That would make you an accomplice. You'd be in deep yogurt if you were caught."

He nodded. The misery solidified into a hard ball with a sloshing core. He felt sick. Moe'd said he'd hurt Isa if Rick didn't go along with his plan.

"I don't care about that. It's...well...people could get hurt. You know?"

She studied him for a long minute. "How hurt?"

He shrugged.

The ice clinked in her tea glass while she took a sip and thought it over. "You want out of it?"

"Yeah." Like, man, did he ever. "How?"

"Tell him no. It'll be hard, but you have to stand up to bullies like that, else they never leave you alone. They get you one time, they got you forever. Know what I mean?"

His throat tightened. He nodded.

"Tell him you won't do it and that if he doesn't leave you alone, you'll have to get help." She paused. "You have to tell your sister—"

"No." He shook his head vehemently. "It would scare her. I can't. She'd hate me," he finished. The tears burned his eyeballs. He was going to cry right here. *Aww, man, don't.*

"Tell Harrison. He'll know what to do. Can you do that?"

"I'll think about it." His voice had sunk low. He could hardly speak. Harrison would be disgusted. He'd send him away, or worse, let him stay but wish he was gone. *Aww, man.*

Maggie gave him one of her no-nonsense stares. "Tell him."

Harrison would hate him, too. "Life's a bitch," he muttered, swamped by self-pity.

"And then you die," Maggie finished in her cheerfully caustic manner.

He sniffed, rubbed his nose, blinked his eyes. "Yeah. Got any rat poison?"

"Nope. Don't have any rats, just a bunch of clowns in this house. Weirdest bunch of 'em I ever saw."

Isa heard the laughter when she opened the door. It gave her a pleasant shock. It sounded like a happy house, a place where people laughed. She clutched the bag of groceries tighter as emotion gripped her.

"Hi, what's so funny?" she asked, setting the bag on the kitchen counter. Maggie and Rick were having a fine time, it seemed. In spite of her worries, her heart felt lighter.

Rick was happy here. So was she. Harrison didn't seem to mind having them, and Maggie had adjusted to their presence.

Paradise. Almost. *She* was the snake in the grass.

"Uh, nothing," her brother replied in his usual informative manner. He ducked his head.

"Private joke. You'd have had to be there," Maggie added.

Casting a fond glance at the other two, Isa set her purse aside and put the fruit and salad vegetables away. They were going through so much fresh stuff because of the heat that it was hard to keep up. It was too hot to cook.

So far August was hotter than July had been, and July had set new records for the duration of high temperatures.

"Harrison will be late tonight. He and Ken and Mr. Merry are having a conference call on the state of the economy."

"How are things going?" Maggie asked. "Should I be looking for a new job?"

"Please, don't even joke about it," Isa implored. "I'd shoot myself."

"My nephew designs jewelry for Harrison."

"Firebird? Tall, lean as a wolf, cheekbones to die for?"

Maggie nodded. "The business is doing well?"

"Yes, it's fine. I've met Jackson. The Firebird designs are stunning and our most popular."

"Not Indian." Maggie snorted in disdain.

"Turquoise and silver have a limited market. His use of other natural stones expands the base. His signature pieces are exquisite. He did a fire sapphire-and-diamond pendant that I'd sell my soul to have. Unfortunately, the jewelry is worth more than that."

Rick stood abruptly. "I, uh, think I'll take a swim." He shuffled down the hall and into his room.

Isa gazed after him, then her smile reappeared. "I talked Mr. Merry into a line of fine jewelry for his stores. The curmudgeon—that's Mr. Parker, my boss— was impressed."

"Good," Maggie said. She leaned close. "Go swim with your brother. I think he needs to talk. But don't push," she added.

"I won't." Isa went to her room and changed to a swimsuit. Out on the patio, she dropped a towel on a chair and crossed the hot patio to the pool.

Maggie called goodbye on her way out before Isa dived in.

Rick, who'd been swimming laps, pulled himself up on the side and waved to Maggie. The two exchanged glances, then solemn smiles. Isa wondered what secrets they shared.

She swam for twenty minutes, then Rick ducked her. She thrashed after him, starting a game of tag. For the first time in years, they played and laughed with each other. After a while, she sat on the side and dangled her legs in the water.

That was where Harrison found them when he got home. "Be out in a sec," he called, heading for the bedroom.

Isa went to the kitchen and prepared tall glasses of iced tea and heaping bowls of Chinese chicken salad for them. She added a basket of crisp flatbread called "bark" by the locals.

Harrison was in the water when she returned to the patio with their supper. She set the table, then tilted the umbrella for maximum shade. The sun would be gone behind the mountains soon. Watching the twilight from the patio was one of her favorite moments. Watching her husband was another.

He emerged from the pool as fluid and sleek as a seal. Her heart gave a painful hitch as he toweled off. She could love a man like him. It would be so easy....

Rick splashed out of the pool, shedding water like a happy puppy. Droplets sprayed over her as he flipped a towel behind his back and sawed it back and forth. He flopped into a chair in that boneless way the young had.

"Madam." Harrison held her chair.

She settled into it, felt his kiss on her head and lifted her face to his. He kissed her mouth, a quick kiss with a lot of promise in it. His smile was sensuous, his gaze playful.

"So, how did the conference call with Merry go?" she asked.

"Perfect."

They discussed the future while they ate. Even Rick joined in, asking questions that clearly showed his keen intellect. Isa was proud of her two men.

Later, they swam and played games in the pool. After that, they watched a storm over the Sierras, a summer storm full of heat lightning and sweeping sheets of rain. The tall peaks captured the clouds so that the storm didn't reach the valley where they watched the awesome display of nature.

Isa glanced at Harrison in the fading twilight. His face seemed sculpted from luminous stone, his eyes from some dark, undiscovered gem that gleamed with magic light.

It wasn't real. She looked at them as if she were an alien observing the scene from afar—the stormy hills, the sage-dotted valley, the snug house, the tranquil pool, the happy family. It wasn't real.

Feelings she'd fought so hard to suppress rushed over her like lightning zigzagging across the far peaks. She was in love with her husband, oh, so terribly in love.

Chapter Thirteen

"I'm going to the office this morning," Harrison announced at breakfast on Saturday. He refilled his and Isa's coffee mugs. "What are you two doing today?"

"I have to work," Rick told him. "We got a big shipment of stuff yesterday. It has to be unpacked and inventoried."

"How about you?" Harrison asked when Isa remained quiet. He steeled himself against her allure. After the session in her office yesterday, he'd decided not to let passion get the upper hand last night.

She'd surprised him. As soon as they were in bed, she'd turned to him with an urgency that had been gratifying. Yeah, it was nice to be wanted, but he wondered what scheme she was hatching. She had seemed almost desperate.

Later, her sleep had been restless and more than once he'd been awakened by low mumbled sounds of protest from her. Perhaps her conscience was bothering her. Ha. She hadn't blinked an eye when she'd forced him into marriage.

Still, there were undercurrents of emotion between them that he didn't understand. He wondered if she was trying to make him fall in love with her. With the life she had here, compared to her former existence, she'd be a fool not to try to figure out a way she could stay.

By forgetting to use protection, he might have given her the perfect excuse. If she were pregnant, he wouldn't let her leave, not with his child.

His personal life was in a hell of a mess.

"I have some shopping to do. Then...I don't know."

"Come have lunch with me," he invited on an impulse. Maybe he'd find out what plan she'd been concentrating on so furiously the past few days. "I'll be finished by noon. We could go to that little place you like. How about you, Rick? Will you be finished by then?"

"Uh, yeah. I think so. But, uh, I gotta...I've got things to do." He put his cereal bowl in the dishwasher. "See you guys later." He loped out without looking at either of them.

A long beat of silence followed his departure.

"Something's wrong," Isa said.

He felt a tightening in his gut. "Like what?"

She shook her head. "I don't know."

"With us?"

She looked at him, startled. Color ran under her skin. "No. At least...I mean..."

"Nothing more than usual?" he suggested wryly.

He waited while she sipped the hot coffee. He noticed her fingers trembled on the mug. It made him nervous, this anxiety of hers. Like maybe she was anxious for him to be gone. Was she meeting someone else?

It was damned odd to be so certain of a woman when they made love and to be so uncertain the rest of the time. They'd been married almost four months and he was no closer to understanding her than when they'd met.

"A man could get frustrated dealing with a woman," he mentioned when she didn't speak. He suppressed an impulse to shake the truth out of her.

Her smile disclosed nothing of her thoughts. "Lots of men seem to feel that way about women."

Seeing he wasn't going to win points in discussing the battle of the sexes, he went back to her original statement. "So what do you think is wrong?"

"It's Rick."

She looked at him, her green eyes luminous with worry. It made him want to leap tall buildings for her. What a fool. Going soft in the head over a woman was the last thing he needed right now.

"He seems to be doing okay. He told me he liked the job. His boss said the boy was a fine worker."

"No, it isn't that. It's...well, it's probably nothing. I think he said something to Maggie. I'll talk to her Monday."

"You want me to talk to him?"

Isa clasped her hands around the warm porcelain and watched the steam rise from the coffee. Rick was her responsibility. She'd forced Harrison to take them into his home. That was the extent of their deal. Harrison had already done a lot for Rick.

"Would you mind?" she asked.

"No." He leaned close, his smile mocking. "A man will do anything for his woman, don't you know?"

She looked away as a bottomless pit opened inside her. He was baiting her. She'd sensed his wariness of her increasing lately. He distrusted her now, but he accepted her in his life. He'd hate her when she told him the truth.

The only thing he wanted from her was sexual gratification. Humiliation burned in her. She'd turned to him as soon as they went to bed, needing the security of his arms around her. Then she'd wanted more.

It scared her, this wanting…as if she depended on him, as if she couldn't live without him. She didn't like being in love. It was too scary.

Harrison cupped his hand under her chin and lifted her face to his. His expression was hard. "What are you scheming about now? I can almost hear the wheels turning. Don't think you can wind your way around me like a vine smothering an oak." His hand tightened. "I can easily tear you out by the roots and toss you on the fire."

Long after he'd left, she sat in the kitchen, her hands to her forehead until her heart settled into a steady beat again. Harrison knew something was wrong. He knew.

The ringing of the telephone interrupted her tortured reverie.

"This is Martha Addleson," a friendly voice said.

The social worker. Isa's heart went frantic again. "Hello, Martha. How are you?" she asked.

"Fine. Is Rick in? I have his grades here and I wanted to congratulate him on a job well done."

"No, he had to work today."

"Oh? Where?"

Isa wondered if it was okay for Rick to have a job. She hadn't thought to ask. "Reno Wholesale Imports.

It's in the same building as Harrison's company. Is that all right?''

"Yes, of course. He just didn't mention it when I talked to him on the phone last time."

"I see. Does he seem to be adjusting okay?" Worry gnawed at her. Something was definitely bothering him. Maybe he'd shared it with the case worker.

"Yes. His teachers report he did well last term. He's made a couple of friends, one of them a girl. That's usually a good sign," Martha told her, laughing. "He seems to have settled in very well. Sometimes it's simply a matter of getting away from the influence of bad companions. Rick also admires your husband. Harrison is a fine role model. I understand they worked together on a car this summer."

"Yes, they did."

"Excellent. Well, I have to go. Tell Rick I'm proud of him and that I'll talk to him next week."

"Right. I will. 'Bye."

Isa hung up, her mind racing with half thoughts that flitted off before she had time to analyze them. There was trouble. She could sense it the way a wild creature senses danger.

She continued to worry while she showered and dressed for her shopping trip. Maybe she was overreacting. With her guilt and indecision over confessing all to Harrison, she was probably paranoid about the whole situation. Rick was fine most of the time. Just once in a while he seemed to withdraw again.

A blast of dry heat hit her like a puff from a bellows when she went out to her car. She cranked up the engine and turned on the air-conditioning full blast.

It was the heat, she decided on her way to town. She and Rick weren't used to this weather. That was why he was tense and she was leaping to conclusions. Yes, it was the heat.

The end-of-summer sales were good, but her heart wasn't in it. She bought underwear, which had been her main objective, added two slacks outfits, a blouse and a vest, then called it quits.

Glancing at her watch, she saw it was a little early for lunch. She'd go to the office and do some work while she waited for her men.

Her heart gave a gigantic leap.

Her men. She realized how very much she wanted that to be true. She thought of how Harrison would react if she confessed she'd fallen in love with him. Not that he would believe her. He'd probably laugh.

"Harrison, I'm out of here. See you Monday."

Harrison looked at the clock after Ken left. A little after eleven. He'd been working steadily for three hours. He threw down the pen and stretched, giving a huge yawn.

Propping his feet on the desk, his hands behind his head, he contemplated his life. In many ways, it was as good as it had ever been.

He had a warm, exciting woman in his bed every night—just thinking about her turned him on—and the business was going well, so he should be satisfied. He wasn't. There was more to life than sex and money. He wanted...hell, he didn't know... Forever? Commitment? Vows of undying love?

Those were things women usually demanded from men. But not his wife. Now there was a nice piece of irony. When he finally met the woman of his dreams, or so he'd thought that first month, she'd turned out to be a schemer and blackmailer, a con artist of the first degree. He glanced toward heaven.

"Is this some kind of a joke?" he demanded. "A test?"

Yeah, right. He was like old Job—his faith in love and marriage, as exemplified by his parents, was being tested to the limit. His marriage was beyond the limits and definitely failing the test.

He ignored the swirl of useless fury at being taken in by her innocent face and haunting eyes. He still hadn't penetrated the obscuring mist and figured her out. He was beginning to think he never would. So where did that leave them?

At an impasse.

Restless, he stood and headed out the door. He'd go down and see how Rick was doing. He took the stairs instead of the elevator, since they opened onto a corridor next to the storage area where the teenager worked.

On the first floor, the offices were dark, the doors all closed and locked. He let himself out a side exit and headed around the building. Just as he reached the corner near the loading dock, he heard the heavy metal door open.

"Hello, Ricky-boy," a voice said.

Harrison stopped instinctively. He didn't like the tone of the person who'd spoken. It had been the voice of a bully, one sure of his hold over another.

"Moe." Rick sounded startled. "What are you doing here?"

"Well, I got to wondering about things—like whether or not you'd meet me like I told you."

"I told you I wouldn't," Rick replied. The bottom dropped out of his stomach. "You shouldn't be here."

"I cruised the block several times. You're by yourself.'' Moe pulled a knife from his pocket and flicked a button. The blade leapt from its casing. He proceeded to casually clean his nails with the sharp steel. ''Now did you lie to me, Ricky-boy, or were you, like, mistaken?''

''There's another guy here. He has an office upstairs.'' Rick kept his eyes on the knife, mesmerized by the way the hot sun gleamed off the blade as Moe worked on his nails. He thought of it piercing his skin, slicing into his gut.

Fear grabbed him by the throat. He didn't want to die. He had school ahead of him. There was a girl he'd met on a field trip into the desert. He swallowed and squared his shoulders.

''I'm not going to let you do it, Moe,'' he said, sounding a lot stronger than he felt.

''Do what?''

''Rob the place.''

Moe assumed a fake innocence. ''Me? Nah, you got it wrong, kid. I've got pals in Carson City. I've been with them all morning, all afternoon, tonight, too.'' He grinned.

Rick shook his head. ''I'm not going to leave the door unlocked. I'm not going to let you do this.''

''You got a sweet-looking sister,'' Moe said, changing his manner to a serious, confidential one. ''I'd hate to see anything happen to her, you know? Be a shame if her brakes failed on the way home one night. Her pretty face could get all broken up. I saw that happen once. Yeah, a friend's wife got her face all smashed up—''

''I'm not going to help you,'' Rick interrupted.

''I figured you might get cold feet. That's why I came by early. We're going to do the job now, you and me.

How about that, huh? Let's go inside.'' He pushed a battered cowboy hat off his forehead.

"No."

"Ricky, Ricky," Moe chided.

He spread his hands as if helpless to understand this attitude. Sunbeams danced off the honed blade. Rick held his ground. A man had to take a stand for what was right. Moe would never let him go if he hooked him into this.

A man had to be strong. Rick swallowed the knot of fear. He had to show Isa he could be trusted, that she'd been right about him. He had to show Harrison he was a man.

"Actually, I'm not really interested in the import junk. I thought we'd take a little trip upstairs. Know anything about your brother-in-law's business, kid? Jewelry-making. That's always fascinated me. All those expensive rocks. That's what gems are. People pay money for little pieces of rock."

Rick thought of Harrison up in his office, unaware of the danger. If he should run into Moe in the hall or catch him in the act, he'd try to stop him.

The knife gleamed as Moe worked on his other hand. He was ambidextrous and liked to show off. He could throw the knife with either hand and hit a target dead on from several feet away.

Rick glanced around for a weapon. Nothing. He'd come outside carrying a load of flattened boxes for the dumpster. He didn't even have the razor he used to slit the boxes open with him. It was inside on a shelf. There was nothing on the loading dock but the cardboard he'd dropped upon spotting the man he'd once thought of as his friend.

"I'm not going to let you in."

"You think you're some kind of hero?" Moe sneered.

When he took a step forward, Rick kicked the pile of used boxes at him. Moe sidestepped. It gave Rick just enough time to jump inside the door and slam it behind him. He heard the automatic lock click into place. His knees turned to jelly.

For the first time, he realized sweat was running down his face. Fear sweat. He'd felt it once before, the night of the warehouse burglary that had landed him in jail. At least he wasn't a patsy this time.

He mopped his face on the sleeve of his T-shirt and headed for the stairs. He had to warn Harrison, then call the police.

A feeling of lightness came over him. Yeah, he'd tell everything. He should have from the first. Moe wasn't a friend, just a bully who tried to force others to do his dirty work.

"Hey, Ricky," Moe shouted through the door. "Guess who's here? Your sister just arrived. She's wearing a red outfit. Umm, she looks good enough to eat."

Rick froze. Was this a trick?

Isa hesitated after getting out of the car. There was a man on the loading dock. She thought she'd seen Rick when she turned the corner, but he wasn't in sight now.

Her nerves tightened. Honestly, she was becoming paranoid. The guy leaning against the railing cleaning his fingernails was only a few years older than Rick. He probably worked at the import warehouse, too. Anyway, he looked perfectly harmless.

Rick was right. She was a worrywart.

She slung her purse strap over her shoulder and

climbed the steps to the loading dock. "Hello," she called. "Did I see Rick here a moment ago?"

The guy glanced up, then ducked his head. "Yeah. He went inside to get something. Hey, Rick, your sister wants to see you," he yelled at the door.

Isa frowned at the untidy pile of flattened cardboard. She'd have to walk over the mess or very close to the shy young man to get to the door.

"Uh, there's a buzzer," she pointed out, stopping a couple of feet from the boxes. "Ring that, and he'll come to the door."

"Go ahead," he invited. He stepped back in the corner of the railing, keeping his head down so his cowboy hat shielded most of his face.

The sense of unease grew stronger. She knew this guy. "Moe," she said before she could stop herself. "What are you doing here? You were in—"

"Jail?" he supplied. "I'm out on bail."

She knew at once he'd jumped bail. She looked at the knife in his hand. It was menacing, although he was merely using it to pare his nails. He was the one who'd visited Rick yesterday. He was the friend who'd gotten Rick into trouble. All her maternal instincts rose in a cloak of fury.

"I want you to stay away from Rick," she told him. "If you don't, I'll notify the authorities. Does your parole officer know where you are?"

Harrison beat a trail back the way he'd come. He used his key to let himself back in the building as quietly as he could. As soon as he took care of the hoodlum out there, he was going to wring his sweet wife's neck. If she didn't get herself killed first.

"Rick," he said.

The teenager jerked around, his eyes wild. His hand was on the door.

"Don't go out there," Harrison ordered.

"I have to. He's got Isa."

Harrison ignored the lurch in his chest. "We need a plan. I think we can take him by surprise if we storm the door together." He spotted a pile of throw rugs. He grabbed one and tossed another to Rick. "Wrap your left arm and use it as a shield from the knife."

"That's imported, handwoven stuff," Rick said as if this was important information.

Harrison grinned, startling the teenager. "Yeah, well, better them than us. We'll pay for the damages," he added dryly. "Ready on three?"

Rick nodded. It hit him that he and Harrison were going to rush into danger together. They were going to save Isa and stop Moe. Like some kind of SWAT team. He gulped and nodded.

Harrison grinned again. Excitement beat through Rick. He and his brother-in-law were going to make like heroes. It freaked him out. It made him proud.

"One."

Rick wrapped the rug around his left arm and took hold of the doorknob with his right hand. He nodded at Harrison.

"Two. Three. Hit it," Harrison said in a growl.

Rick turned the knob and threw all his weight against the door. He and Harrison exploded onto the loading dock.

Moe was startled, but only for a second. He struck out with the knife. Rick saw Harrison had his left arm ready. A gaping slash appeared in the imported rug. His boss was going to have a fit. They were a special buy.

Moe flung himself headfirst into Harrison. Rick

turned to waylay the bully. The cardboard skittered underfoot. He flung his hand out to catch the banister, but he was already going down. He felt a sharp pain in his right arm, then blood hit him in the face. He heard Isa scream his name.

Isa stared at the tangle of bodies struggling on the loading dock. Harrison had Moe's wrist, but he was working at a disadvantage. The cardboard had shifted when Moe charged and all three men went down in a heap, Rick on the bottom, then Harrison, then Moe, on top and wielding the knife.

Rick was hurt. His left arm was trapped under the two fighting men while blood spurted from his right arm and onto his and Harrison's shirts.

Moe jerked his arm back, freeing it. She saw his muscles flex mightily and knew he was going to stab Harrison. Fury exploded inside her.

Time slowed.

The distance was two steps. She made one of them. Moe's arm had started its downward arc. Second step. The blade was halfway to Harrison's throat. She brought her purse around and forward. The knife had less than six inches to go. She thrust with all her might.

The knife rammed into the soft leather.

Harrison pushed Isa aside and shoved Moe off. Bringing his knee up, he caught the hoodlum on the edge of his jaw. Moe's head flipped back from the blow. Harrison struck again, a blow to the side this time. Moe grunted and fell to the dock.

In a flash, Harrison had Moe pinned with his hands behind his back. The knife was now in Harrison's grip. "Move and you'll be sorry," he advised.

"Listen, man, this was a mistake," Moe whined. "I wasn't doing anything—"

"The mistake was yours." Harrison settled a knee heavily into the small of Moe's back and cut the strap from Isa's purse. He secured the hoodlum's wrists. "I'm going to let you get up," he said. "Do it nice and slow, so I don't get nervous with this blade, understand?"

"Yeah, man. Take it easy."

Isa checked her husband over when he stood. He wasn't hurt. All the blood came from Rick. She knelt by her brother. He held a rug against his arm as a pressure bandage. "Let me see."

He gladly allowed her to take over.

"How is he?" Harrison asked. He motioned Moe over against the wall, keeping himself between the man and the other two.

"The wound is long, but not deep. He'll be fine." She pressed the makeshift bandage over the wound and smiled at Rick. All the love she'd ever felt for him gathered inside her. She hugged him fiercely.

He hugged her back with his good arm. "I'm sorry," he said. "It was my fault. I should have told you about Moe, that he was in town—"

She shushed him. "It's okay. It wasn't your fault." She got to her feet. Her legs were a little wobbly. "I'll call the police."

"Good idea."

At her husband's words, she turned to him, her heart in her throat. He had blood and dirt on his shirt and in his hair. A bruise was forming under his eye. She thought he was the handsomest man alive.

She had to touch him. Just once. She laid her hand on his arm. "Thank you."

His eyes blazed over her. She drew back, confused

by the fury she saw in him. "The police," he reminded her.

She got the key to the back door from Rick and went inside. Within two minutes of her call, two cruisers howled into the parking lot. She leaned against the railing and sighed as four policemen pounded up the steps like the A Team on a major bust. Men always had to make such a drama out of things.

"Wow, that was really something, wasn't it?" Rick giggled like a kid at Christmas.

Isa smiled. He was feeling the effects of adrenaline and the shot of painkiller the nurse had given him before the emergency-room doctor had stitched up his arm. He talked all the way to the house.

Once there, he went to his room, fell across the bed and conked out. Isa removed his shoes and spread a throw over him. He drew his feet up on the bed and turned so his hurt arm rested on the pillow beside his head.

For a long minute, she stood beside the bed, watching him sleep. She'd never forget him and Harrison bursting out the door and overtaking Moe. "My heroes," she murmured.

Bending, she kissed her brother's cheek and smoothed his hair. He smiled. "Love ya," he murmured the way he used to years ago when he'd been a child and she'd read him a bedtime story.

Tears filmed her eyes. She left the room and closed the door behind her. Restless, she paced the kitchen, waiting for Harrison to finish with the police and come home.

She remembered they hadn't had a chance to go to lunch with all the excitement at the loading dock. She shook her head, feeling close to laughing or crying, she didn't know which.

When she heard the garage door open, then close, her heart went into a dive to her toes, then beat like mad.

Checking the cupboards, she decided on tomatoes stuffed with tuna salad. She was busy when Harrison came in. "Hi," she said, glancing at him, then away.

She wanted to rush to his arms, run her hands over him to make sure he was really okay, then take him to their room....

"How'd it go with the local authorities?" she asked on a light note.

"No problems. Moe will be charged for attempting to corrupt a minor or something like that, then shipped back to Oregon for trial on armed robbery. He'd skipped bail."

"I thought maybe he had." A tremor ran through her. "I'm glad he's in custody. Will Rick have to testify against him?"

"Probably. We'll go with him. He won't be alone," Harrison added as worry flicked through her eyes and was gone.

She paused for a second, looking pensive. He wondered what she was thinking. As usual, her face gave nothing away.

"Lunch," she announced. She placed their plates on the counter and poured tall glasses of iced tea.

When she took her place, he sat next to her. "This is nice," he said. "A quiet lunch, prepared by my wife, just the two of us."

He watched closely and noticed the tremor in her hands. She wasn't eating very much, but was mostly moving the food around on her plate. Her stillness—

that deep inner quiet that hid her soul and was somehow mournful—bothered him.

"That was good," he said when he finished.

She'd eaten about three bites. When she raised her glass to drink, he realized she was trembling from head to toe. He muttered a curse, angry with himself that he hadn't detected her distress before now.

"Come on," he said, taking her arm.

"What is it?" She looked at him in alarm, then away.

"You're having aftershocks," he told her. "I know the very thing for that."

She went with him…reluctantly…but she went. "I have to talk to you." She sounded desperate.

"Take your clothes off," he ordered when they reached their bedroom. "First we're going to get comfortable, then we'll talk."

Chapter Fourteen

Isa stared at Harrison's back. He was bent over the hot tub, adjusting the temperature of the water. When he was satisfied, he flicked a switch on the wall. The water swooshed through the jets and foamed into bubbles.

Sitting naked in a hot tub didn't seem the best approach to what she had to tell him. She clenched her arms across her body, but nothing could dispel the trembling that seemed to be overtaking her. Now that the emergency was over, she was falling apart. No wonder Harrison thought she was a basket case.

He turned around and saw her standing in the middle of the room. "Need some help?" Without further ado, he started removing her clothing.

"Are you getting in, too?"

"No. Perhaps another time," he added, giving her an odd perusal that made her tremble more. There was a determined gleam in his eyes. She didn't know what it meant, and she was so tired of walking a tightrope of guilt and fear.

She desperately needed to be alone. She didn't know how much longer she could control the waves of emotion that swept over her. Images of a knife flashing bright and hot in the sun appeared every time she blinked her eyes.

Harrison could have been killed because of her, because she'd self-righteously involved him in her family problems when she'd had no right to do so. She'd been wrong, and he'd nearly paid with his life.

He unbuttoned her blouse and slipped it from her.

She didn't think she could confess all her sins sitting naked in a hot tub. "I think...we need..."

"Some peace and quiet," he supplied in a husky murmur. He kissed her shoulder while he removed her bra. "Did I ever tell you how lovely you are?"

"No...yes...when we..."

"Make love, yes." He chuckled as he whisked her shoes and slacks and underpants off. "I think it other times, too."

Tears rose, urgent and burning, to her eyes. She blinked them away. She had to stay calm, rational. She had to...had to tell him he'd been right about his father....

He rubbed her shoulders, massaging the muscles that were clenched as hard as lead pipe. "Relax," he ordered softly.

Swooping, he lifted her into his arms and walked across the carpet to the tub. There, he set her on her feet on the first step. The warmth crept over her chilled flesh.

"Sit," he ordered.

She did as he said.

"I'll be right back." He left the room.

She sank into the bubbling warmth up to her neck and let her head rest on the slanted back of the tub. Freed of his presence and the need to hold on to her control, she let her mind drift.

She imagined how different life would be if Harrison were to love her. If, at the end of their year, he would refuse to let her go. Perhaps, if she didn't tell him about her father...

A knot settled in her throat. She couldn't accept their marriage on that basis. To build a life, then see it destroyed when he found out the truth would be foolish.

The tears pressed closer. She fought them off.

"Here."

She opened her eyes. Harrison held a towel ready for her. She stepped out with the weariness of a mountain climber who'd failed to reach the top and had only the long trek to the bottom of the mountain before her. He dried her off over her protest, then wrapped her in her warm nightgown and robe.

After urging her into an easy chair, he propped her feet on an ottoman. He handed her a mug of steaming liquid. It was an effort to reach up and take it.

The scent of spices wafted under her nose as she lifted the mug. "What is this?"

"Hot tea with a spot of buttered rum. Drink up." He guided her hand to her mouth.

She took a sip.

"Another drink," he encouraged.

The warmth went all the way to her toes. She took another sip, then another. When she finished, a delicious lassitude seeped through her. "Are you trying to get me tipsy?"

He sat on the ottoman, her feet snuggled between his

thighs. "Maybe I'm trying to take the edge off that keen mind of yours." To her surprise, he displayed a deck of cards. "How about a game?" He cut the deck into halves and fanned the cards on his knee.

"Now?" Her voice cracked. She cleared it self-consciously. She had to confess before she lost her nerve. "I have something to tell you—"

"Let's play Truth. Whoever wins the cut gets to ask a question. The other has to answer truthfully."

He was in a strange mood. Perhaps it would be better to indulge him. Later, when she could gauge his temper, she'd tell all. Then she had a favor to ask of him.

"All right," she agreed. "Aces high?"

"Yes." He laid the deck on his knee. "You go first."

She cut the cards and looked at the bottom one. A ten.

He cut and got a seven. She'd won the first cut. She tried to think of something.

"You like Rick, don't you?" she finally asked.

His dark brows went up slightly, but he nodded. "Very much. He has the makings of a fine man."

Relief washed through her. "You were both wonderful today. I didn't know what was going on when you crashed through the door like a demolition team."

He laughed, a quiet chuckle that reached right down into her soul. Her throat closed as longing slashed through her.

"Next cut," he said. He went first. His jack beat her five. He studied her for a long minute as if searching for the precise question he wanted to ask. "Why did you leap in front of Moe's knife?"

Again he surprised her. She tried to bring her thoughts together, but the words seemed to run in every direction with no logic. She put a hand to her forehead to shield her eyes from his candid gaze. "Well, be-cause...I thought...he was going to hurt you. He was trying to stab you."

He reached out and brought her hand down to her lap. "I want to see your face."

The tension increased. She sat up straight, then moved her hand away from him. He let her go. She pulled her feet onto her chair and wrapped her arms over her knees, pulling them against her body, hiding from him as if he could see her guilty heart through the clothing that covered it.

She felt exposed, vulnerable to his male determina-tion. She realized when it came to force of will she was no match for his driving strength. "What do you want?"

The faintest tremor entered her voice.

He fanned the deck, then gave her first choice on cutting the cards. She picked up the top four or five.

"You saved my life today. It's hard to think of the proper words to thank a person for that," he said con-versationally.

She stared at the ace. "It was nothing. I didn't think about what I was doing. I just reacted."

"It was a brave thing to do," he murmured. His ex-pression was solemn. He picked up one card. "Remind me to buy you a new purse."

"That's okay. You needn't."

He flashed his card. An ace. "A draw," he said when she held hers out. They cut again. He won.

"After we had Moe tied up, you looked me over before going to see about Rick's injury. Why?"

She closed her eyes and saw the blood on his shirt, the flash of the knife in the hot sun. Time stopped as she relived the danger, throwing herself forward, reaching out, afraid, so afraid he would be hurt.

"I saw Moe slash at you with the knife," she finally said in a harsh whisper. She licked her parched lips and looked at him. "There was blood on your shirt." She shook her head while the knot of fear crept into her throat.

Afraid. She'd been so afraid for him.

He lowered his eyelashes to sexy levels as he studied her with a steadfastness that made her uneasy, as if he didn't believe what she said.

"I wanted to make sure you weren't cut," she ended.

"I wasn't."

She nodded. Words failed her. She'd thought she would die when Harrison and Rick had burst through that door like a couple of Power Rangers to the rescue. She giggled suddenly.

"What's so funny?" he demanded softly.

She told him. "But the cardboard caused you to slip. That scared me." She stopped and looked at him helplessly, caught up in her fear for him once more.

He touched her cheek, rubbed along her jaw and under her chin. "I was scared, too. I was afraid he'd hurt you before we could stop him." He shuffled the cards absently.

"It's strange to have someone worry—" She stopped.

"Yes. That's what's nice about being married—couples are there for each other…through good times and bad, in sickness and health…" He held the deck out to her.

She ignored it. She had to tell him the truth about their past. "I have to tell you something." Each word hurt her throat as she spoke. "About the mining claim."

If he was surprised by the change of subject, he didn't show it. "We can discuss that later. There are more important things right now. It's your cut."

She shook her head, beyond games at the moment. Emotion rushed up from her heart. She was going to cry. Please, no, don't, don't, don't...

"No, I have to tell you," she insisted, not meeting his eyes. She hugged her knees close to her body, locking herself in, holding her aching heart together.

He picked a card and held it between both hands.

"I talked to Mr. Parker," she said.

Again he appeared surprised at the subject. He held the cards out to her. She took one.

Isa stared at the diamond pattern on the back of the card she held and told her husband the entire conversation and all it had disclosed to her.

"That's why you've been so quiet since the party. I thought Helen might have done something that hurt you. I saw she was trying to cut you out, then you reversed the situation on her. I was proud of you."

He apparently didn't understand what she was telling him. She tried again. "Rick and I have no claim...no rights at all where you or the mine is concerned."

"That's why my father filed the second time in his name only. Your father had signed over his share of the mine."

"Yes."

"I had a hard time believing Dad would cheat anyone, but it was beginning to look that way."

"Yes," she said steadily. "It was my father who lied from the first. I shouldn't have believed him."

"It doesn't matter." There was pity in his gaze.

"Please don't be kind." She managed a faint smile. "It only makes things harder."

"A husband and wife can discuss anything."

That was easy for him to say. He, male that he was, believed he could control the world. She knew it wasn't so simple. He turned over his card. A king. He tugged hers out of her hand and held it beside his. A queen.

"Don't you see? I forced you into marriage. I thought that claim gave me the right. I used it to justify every plan I made. I came here with the intent of blackmailing you."

"That was rather obvious. I fell for your scheme hook, line and sinker, didn't I?" He laid the deck aside.

"Yes," she said glumly. She hesitated. "I don't blame you for hating me."

The silence burned between them.

"I don't hate you."

She ignored him. He was being gallant, and she couldn't bear it. She had to get the rest out. "I'll get out of your life as soon as possible."

He gave her a hard stare, but said nothing.

"I'll give you a divorce." She forced her gaze to his, openly pleading now. "Would you let Rick finish out his year? I don't think he'll be a lot of trouble. I know he admires you tremendously. He'll do what you tell him."

To her dismay, he shook his head.

She put her hands over her face. She was going to fall to pieces in front of him. "I have to…have to…" She lunged upward, needing to escape. She got no farther than placing one foot on the carpet.

Harrison caught her to him. The world tilted wildly while he turned with her and sat down, holding her easily with his greater strength while she struggled to be free, to get away before she made a total fool of herself.

"Easy," he said softly. "Don't fight. I'm not going to let you go."

She recovered enough of her poise to quip, "Watch it. I'll drown you with tears if nothing else works."

He tipped her head across his arm and gazed into her eyes. "There are tears in those beautiful eyes. I had wondered if you ever let yourself cry."

"Lots of times," she said flippantly. "You saw them once."

"Shhh." He laid a finger over her lips, then left it there in a caress.

She closed her eyes as longing spiraled deep into her. "Today has been too much, I think. I'm all topsy-turvy inside. Too many emotions rushing about…"

"I know. I have to get to you while your defenses are down. I won the last cut. There's one thing I want to know."

"What?" She kept her eyes closed.

"When you dived in front of that knife, did you know you were in love with me then or did you realize it later?"

She couldn't breathe. Every muscle in her body froze for an instant. She opened her eyes and watched him warily. "What makes you think that…that I…" She took a breath and tried to divert him. "You have a colossal ego."

He smiled slightly. "I suppose I'll have to take the edge off that sharp tongue of yours. The easiest way to do that is to kiss you senseless." He proceeded to do so.

When Isa came up for air, she was clinging to him, his body hard and pulsing against her. She snuggled her head in the groove of his shoulder, unable to meet his knowing gaze.

"Hiding?" There was laughter in his voice.

"Yes." She knew he wasn't going to let it go.

"You have to tell the truth. It's part of the rules. Say you love me, and I'll let you rest. Otherwise, I'll have to keep at it until you confess."

Did he want her total humiliation? "Please," she said on a shaky note. She had no defenses left, no smart remarks, no blank smiles, no shield to hide her heart.

"Yes," he murmured, "to whatever you want. My home, my fortune, such as it is, are yours. There's just one catch—I come with them."

Only the sound of popping bubbles from the hot tub broke the silence.

"Wh-what?" She was afraid to take anything for granted. She might be dreaming.

"My father and I used to go on fishing trips up in the mountains. I finally understand why he wanted to see my mother first thing when we got home. He'd always rush into the house, calling her name. Knowing your woman is there, waiting for you, makes a man feel good." His voice dropped to a husky tone. "That's how you make me feel."

She dared to look at him then. His gaze burned hotly over her. She saw desire, patience, humor, but there was more.

He gave her a stern frown. "I don't want to hear any more talk about our year being up. For us, I want a lifetime. It'll take me that long to get past that poker face of yours and find out what makes you tick." A lazy grin floated over his mouth. "I'm determined to do it, so don't try to stop me."

"You want me to stay?"

"Always."

"Rick, too?"

"Yes, and anybody else you want, as long as I get you at night." His sexy cadence sent a shiver over her.

"Oh."

"What? No sharp-tongued remark? No retort to put me in my place?"

Dazed, she shook her head. She was dreaming. She had to be. Things like this didn't come true in real life.

"There's one thing you have to tell me." Now he was all wistful seriousness. "Do you think you could learn to love me half as much as I love you?"

In the game of life, there comes a time when a woman has to take her chances.

"I think I loved you when we went to Tahoe." It was scary to admit it. It left a woman open, vulnerable to emotional blackmail. "But I thought I shouldn't."

"Because you were going to blackmail me?" His smile widened at her guilty blush. "I was attracted to you from the first. I was also furious at being blackmailed. We had to dance all around the truth before we could admit it, didn't we?"

"Yes."

The gold band sparkled when she lifted her hand to caress his face. He caught her hand in his and kissed the palm, then pressed it to his heart. "I love you. You're the only woman I could imagine marrying, the only one I've ever wanted like that."

"Am I dreaming?" she asked.

"Not a chance. Not until I get done with you, and that won't be for an hour or two or three or..."

She sighed as he nuzzled her neck. Then he settled her more securely across his lap and ravished her. It was the most wonderful sensation in the world. He seemed to like it, too.

When he carried her to their bed, she had no objections.

She had definitely gone soft in the head, she reflected drowsily much later that afternoon. Her husband lay close to her, sound asleep, one leg thrown over hers in sweet intimacy.

Blackmailers must be clear-thinking.

Blackmailers must be ruthless.

She started laughing. She'd been the most muddled blackmailer in history. She'd fallen in love with the victim.

But then, he'd fallen in love with her, too.

So it had evened out in the end.

* * * * *

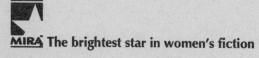

Take 4 bestselling love stories FREE

Plus get a FREE surprise gift!

Share in the joy of yuletide romance with brand-new
stories by two of the genre's most beloved writers

DIANA PALMER

and

JOAN JOHNSTON

in

LONE STAR CHRISTMAS

Diana Palmer and Joan Johnston share their favorite
Christmas anecdotes and personal stories in this
special hardbound edition.

Diana Palmer delivers an irresistible spin-off of her
LONG, TALL TEXANS series and Joan Johnston crafts an
unforgettable new chapter to **HAWK'S WAY** in this wonderful
keepsake edition celebrating the holiday season. So
perfect for gift giving, you'll want one for yourself...and
one to give to a special friend!

Available in November at your favorite retail outlet!

Only from

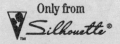

Bestselling author

Joan Johnston

continues her wildly popular miniseries with an
all-new, longer-length novel

The Virgin Groom

HAWK'S WAY

One minute, Mac Macready was a living legend in
Texas—every kid's idol, every man's envy, every
woman's fantasy. The next, his fiancée dumped him,
his career was hanging in the balance and his future
was looking mighty uncertain. Then there was the
matter of his scandalous secret, which didn't stand a
chance of staying a secret. So would he succumb to
Jewel Whitelaw's shocking proposal—or take cold
showers for the rest of the long, hot summer...?

Available August 1997
wherever Silhouette books are sold.

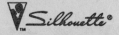